PRIDE OF THE PLAINS

BOOKS IN THE
LIONS OF LINGMERE SERIES

Journey to Freedom
Lion Country
Pride of the Plains

PRIDE OF THE PLAINS

Colin Dann

RED
FOX

A Red Fox Book

Published by Random House Children's Books
20 Vauxhall Bridge Road, London SW1V 2SA

A division of The Random House Group Ltd
London Melbourne Sydney Auckland
Johannesburg and agencies throughout the world

Copyright © Colin Dann 2002

1 3 5 7 9 10 8 6 4 2

First published in Great Britain by Red Fox 2002

Printed in Denmark by Nørhaven Paperback A/S

THE RANDOM HOUSE GROUP Limited Reg. No. 954009

www.randomhouse.co.uk

ISBN 0 09 941126 1

Contents

For Susie

Preface

The sister lionesses, Huru and Kimya, had adapted well to life in the African game park since their release from the animal refuge centre at Kamenza. It was the life they had been intended to lead and was far removed from their upbringing in an English zoo. Their journey from there to Africa was now only a faint memory for them. They had mated with resident lions in the game park and six cubs had been born, three to Huru and three to Kimya. So, together with the four adults, the pride numbered ten animals.

During the wet season the pride had moved on to the plains to take advantage of the abundant prey there. A while later the pride's eldest cub, a male called Moja, had disappeared after being attacked and tossed by a grieving mother elephant. Huru and Kimya searched for him in vain. They didn't know what had happened to him; not even if he was alive or dead.

—1—

Moja

In fact Moja was very much alive. His sturdy frame and thick furry coat had broken his fall. Though bruised and shocked by the elephant's sudden attack, the lion cub scrambled hastily to his feet amongst the soft, tall grass-stems where he had landed with a thump. He hardly knew where he was, but he did know that he was very frightened and must get away from that place as fast as he possibly could. He imagined the thunderous tread of the elephant coming towards him again and he fled, bounding blindly through the thick growth that reached way above his head. He didn't stop running until his panic subsided. Then, as he slowed, he tripped over a root and pitched into a whistling-thorn bush, badly scratching his scalp and one ear. Moja felt very sorry for himself. He didn't stir for a while, not wanting to risk more prickles scraping his skin. But eventually, wide-eyed, he peered through the sharp thorns, hoping to catch a glimpse of some of his family.

There was not a sign of any of them. The landscape was blank and unfamiliar. Moja realised he was lost. At first he was not unduly worried. He was confident that his mother or one of the other adult lions would come looking for him, and it wouldn't be long before he was found. But as time passed and he continued neither to see anyone from his pride, nor even to recognise a sound or a call, he became more and more fretful.

His mother, Huru, was worried. She turned to her sister as they lay with their other cubs around them. 'Did we really look everywhere we could? Did we go far enough?' she asked. 'How is it we didn't catch Moja's scent anywhere or hear his cries?'

Kimya narrowed her eyes as she looked towards the sinking sun on the horizon. A light breeze blew across the plains, refreshing the evening air. 'We should face the fact that Moja has probably been killed,' she said as gently as she could. 'I hope he survived, but the longer he's missing the more likely it is that he hasn't.'

'I still believe he has,' Huru answered quickly, almost before Kimya had finished. She was trying to reassure herself. 'I shan't give up on him yet. And if I can't find him, perhaps Moja will find us.'

Kimya said nothing. She was not optimistic.

'He's a brave little male. He resembles his father,' Huru went on quietly, as though talking to herself. 'He'll be trying even if he's afraid, I know he will.'

Towards dusk, as the sky began to darken, Moja longed to call – to tell his family where he was, that he was lost, that he needed them – but he had the sense to remain silent. He knew that ears other than those of his own pride could be listening. He tried to comfort himself by licking his coat. He wet his paws and wiped them across his face and ear where it smarted. That soothed him a little. Then at last he stirred from the thorn bush, his slightly spotted cub's coat invisible in the darkness. Moja knew he couldn't be seen, and he also knew he mustn't be heard.

'I have to get back to the others somehow,' he told himself. 'If only I knew where they were.' He stood and tried to think of the best way to go. 'Perhaps if I just run back to the place where the elephant dropped me? But . . . but which way is that? How can I tell in the dark?' He sank down on to his haunches and gave way to a frightened whimper. The prospect before him was extremely daunting. 'Oh, *why* didn't they come?' he wailed.

Then he remembered who he was: Moja, the son of Battlescars, the dominant male lion of the entire area. The cub stood erect and shook himself. His round face with its prominent ears took on a proud expression. 'I must be worthy of my father,' he told himself. '*He* wouldn't be skulking here, too jittery to move.' He took a few steps forward, then stopped to listen. There was no sound. He went on further, becoming bolder as time passed.

It was a dark night. The light wind had blown patches of cloud across the sky, screening moon and stars. Then all at once the clouds were gone and a full moon was exposed, its gleam flooding the plains. Shapes and shadows that had been hidden before were suddenly revealed. Now Moja saw that he was not alone as he had thought. Dark figures moved across the landscape; some distant, some closer. The cub paused and looked about him. He could see no familiar lion shapes. He did see zebra grouped together, tossing their heads and flicking their tails as they fed. He saw a giraffe get abruptly to its feet and stretch upwards to reach its favourite foliage on an old acacia. Then a sharp cry behind him made him spin round to search for the cause. A small animal had been caught by a predator, Moja realised, but he could locate neither creature. He trotted forward again, more nervously now, wondering all the while if he was nearing his pride or moving further away from it. A score of different scents were in his nostrils: warm animal smells, perfumes from flowering shrubs, musty odours of dead leaves, twigs and dust. All at once Moja realised he was hungry. He began to take notice of some of the smaller creatures whose own quests for food took them scurrying over the ground. Insects and spiders of all kinds were always plentiful but Moja relished meat.

At the foot of a boulder which formed part of one of the kopjes dotting the plains he found the remains of a meal. Whose meal, Moja didn't know or question. A few scraps of meat amongst the rejected entrails and skin of the abandoned prey were quickly nosed out and eaten by the cub. He bent over the other, more putrid remains, trying to decide if he was hungry enough to sample them.

Suddenly a voice which seemed to spring from nowhere cried, 'Beggars can't be choosers, can they?'

Startled, Moja glanced up, ready to run from the owner of the voice whose food he guessed he had been stealing. A young male lion was looking down at him from the top of the boulder where he had been all along, unknown to Moja. The cub relaxed slightly when he saw the animal was one of his own kind. But he didn't recognise the lion and wasn't sure how to react. 'I – I was hungry,' he explained awkwardly.

'Evidently,' replied the young adult. 'Where's the rest of your pride? You can't be hunting alone?'

'I don't know where they are,' Moja answered frankly. 'I'm lost and I'm trying to find them.'

The young lion slipped from his resting-place. 'I've been watching you,' he said. 'I think I've seen you before.'

Moja showed some surprise. 'How could you?' he asked without thinking. 'I've never seen *you*.'

'Huh! Maybe not. I'm always cautious.' The older animal was amused by Moja's naivety. 'I don't advertise my presence, you know. But I think you're one of the cubs in the big dark-maned males' territory.'

Moja didn't reply. He wondered where this was leading to and if he was, after all, in danger.

The young adult continued. 'Is your father the one with all the scars or is he the one with the blacker mane?'

Moja replied at once now, full of pride. 'I'm Battle-scars's son. He's my father.'

'The two go together, don't they?' the lion mocked him. 'Is your mother the beautiful lioness or the even more beautiful lioness?'

'I don't know what you mean,' Moja said innocently. 'Who are you?'

'Call me Challenger.'

'All right. Anyway, why do you want to know so much – er – Challenger?'

'No reason. Just interest. And with an eye to the future,' the older animal answered enigmatically. He began to prowl around the cub, eyeing him closely. 'You shouldn't be out here alone,' he said. 'It's dangerous. And you're already injured.'

Moja didn't enjoy the close scrutiny but he stood his ground. 'How do you know I was injured?' he asked, thinking of the elephant.

'You're bleeding.'

'Oh, that. I thought you meant—' Moja stopped, unsure how much he ought to give away about himself.

'Meant what?' the lion prompted.

Moja explained reluctantly. 'That's how I got lost,' he finished.

'Well – you're a lucky cub,' Challenger declared. 'I wonder you weren't killed. And your luck's still with you, isn't it?'

'I don't know. Is it?'

'Of course it is. Because you met me. And I can help you, little lion.'

'I – I don't see how,' Moja said uncertainly. He wished he had never seen this strange adult who puzzled him and made him feel uneasy.

'I'm going to look after you,' Challenger told him sweetly, 'while we look for your pride. You're too young and vulnerable to do it alone.'

Moja blinked as he tried to decide if he trusted the older animal. There was something about him that didn't inspire Moja's confidence. And why would he want to bother with another family's cub? On the other hand, if the offer was genuine Moja had more chance of being reunited quickly with his pride than if he continued to search alone.

'I'm sure I know your mother,' Challenger was saying persuasively. 'Did she at one time have a slight limp?'

'I don't know,' Moja answered. 'I can't remember.'

'Of course. You're very young.' Challenger squatted and looked at the cub directly. 'That's why you must take shelter now while I begin the search.'

'But—'

'No "buts",' Challenger insisted. 'We can't go together now. We might miss each other in the dark. There's a good deep hole behind my rock where you can hide. You'll be quite safe in there. Are you still hungry?'

'Yes. A little,' Moja admitted.

'Good. I'll bring you back something in a little while. Something a bit fresher than those leavings you were sniffing at just now. Do you see that hole? You go in there now' – he advanced on the cub who backed obediently – 'and keep still and quiet, like your mother taught you, until I return.'

There was no arguing with this much larger animal who almost propelled Moja into the opening, forestalling any possible dissension by blocking the hole with his body. 'Are you comfortable?' he asked.

'Y-yes,' Moja answered in a small voice.

'All right, then. You sit tight there. You don't want to go wandering off whilst I'm away because then I'd have to come and rescue you again, wouldn't I?'

This time Moja didn't answer. It all sounded reasonable enough but for some reason the cub felt threatened, rather than comforted, by these words.

Challenger waited a moment longer, his eyes unwavering as they met Moja's. Then he turned and ambled away. Moja breathed more freely, even as he realised that he was little more than a prisoner.

—2—

Hostage

Moja's brother Mbili and sister Tatu, and his three cousins Nne, Tano and Sita, continually pestered their mothers about their missing sibling. Moja, the eldest of the cubs by a fraction, was their leader.

'Why doesn't he come back?' Mbili asked Huru.

'Won't you look for him again?'. asked Tatu. 'We miss him.'

'Of course you do. And no more than I do myself,' their mother replied. 'We've searched for him everywhere. I really don't know where else I can go. So I've asked your father to keep his eyes peeled when he's on his travels. Don't worry. I still feel we'll have Moja back with us soon.'

Kimya gave much the same answer to her cubs when they asked, although she was far less sure about Moja's reappearance. She told her mate, Battlescars's brother Blackmane, that she feared the worst. 'A lone cub couldn't last long on the plains, could he?' she reasoned. 'Even if the elephant didn't break every bone in his body.'

Blackmane sighed. 'The longer he's absent the more likely it is that he's dead,' he agreed. 'But my brother and I may find him on our journey to the larger pride. And we need to go soon.' He didn't add 'before the females wander too far off' although that was the purpose of their journey. The brothers still controlled two prides; for several seasons they had been supreme and had met with little resistance. Now as they grew older Battlescars and Blackmane found life more difficult. They were fully stretched. New challenges to their authority appeared with wearying regularity and they were only just able to hold on to their own.

Huru and Kimya were as loyal to their mates as they were to each other. Theirs was a tightly knit pride. The larger pride to the north had begun to unravel. It was older and comprised adult lions of varying ages as well as cubs. Some of the young males were ready to leave while the newly mature females were beginning to show interest in suitors who came from outside their territory. Such changes were in the nature of things: prides broke up, old leaders were toppled. Some prides re-formed, other new ones were created.

Challenger, the young male lion, was aware of all this and he had waited his chance. He knew it would come one day and now he thought he saw a way of making that day arrive. The sister lionesses Huru and Kimya were of special interest to him. On two previous occasions, with the help of his brothers, Challenger had aspired to overthrow the older males Battlescars and Blackmane. The trio had failed because of their youth and inexperience. Challenger's brothers, less bold than he, had come off worst in these encounters and had moved elsewhere. But Challenger hadn't given up and was as ambitious as ever. He kept his sights on the pride from a distance, patiently waiting for a time when the males made one of their periodic treks. Then he intended to steal in and claim one of the sisters for his own. He had the highest opinion of himself and his abilities and reckoned the lioness would need little persuasion to join him.

And now he had an added inducement for the mother lion to stray. He knew where her missing cub was and he alone could take her to him. Moja was the perfect lure. With the cub safely stowed in a place of concealment the young male moved confidently through the darkness towards Huru and Kimya's territory. But he wasn't careless. He had learnt to use the utmost caution whilst he kept the pride in view. He reached a favourite look-out point and waited for daylight.

When dawn broke Challenger was alert at once, scanning the immediate prospect for the group of lions he had watched so regularly. They were very close and he quickly flattened himself against his rocky perch. Battlescars and Blackmane were both present, stretching lazily while some of the cubs played around them. Challenger yawned and backed away. His plan could wait. He had all the time in the world.

As he turned to head for his own base he remembered his promise to bring meat to Moja. A fat green lizard was just emerging into the sunlight from a fissure in the rock. Challenger trapped it with one paw and snapped it up. Then he set off quietly on his return journey.

Moja was eagerly awaiting his meal. He was very hungry indeed and had been looking out for Challenger since the first rays of daylight. He saw the young adult pacing towards him with the lizard clamped in his jaws and ran out to meet him.

'Did you see them? Did you see them?' Moja cried as the lizard was deposited on the ground.

'Eat first,' Challenger said.

Moja smelt the reptile's shiny skin. 'This isn't meat,' he declared.

'Of course it's meat! What do you think it is?'

'I don't know.'

'Taste it then. I've carried it all this way back for you.'

Moja took the prey gingerly between his teeth and bit. It *was* meat and it was still warm, but it tasted strange.

'You'll get used to eating all kinds of things when you have to hunt for yourself,' Challenger told him.

Moja was reminded that at present he didn't because his mother hunted for him. 'Did you see them?' he repeated as he chewed without much enjoyment.

Challenger considered while he licked a paw and drew it through his thickening mane. 'Yes,' he said slowly. 'I saw them. But it wouldn't be safe to take you yet. Your father would attack me.'

'When do we go, then?' Moja asked with his mouth full.

'At dusk. Or – or – a bit later,' Challenger replied airily. 'And when you've eaten that you'd better go back into hiding.'

'But I don't want to,' Moja protested. 'It's dark and smelly and damp. And I want a drink.'

'All right, you can drink. But after that . . .'

'Where can I drink?' Moja asked.

'Use your eyes,' Challenger grunted. 'Plenty of puddles around.' He relented when he saw Moja's crestfallen face. The cub was pretty young to be searching on his own. 'Follow me,' the older animal said more gently. 'I'll find you some water.'

Moja didn't want to follow: he wanted to be along-side. He matched Challenger's pace by trotting two steps to the adult's one. Challenger glanced at him from time to time from the corner of his eye. He noticed that the cub winced every so often. 'Are you in pain?' he queried.

'A few bruises, I think,' Moja panted. 'The elephant hurled me.'

'Yes, you told me. But you're a fine-looking cub,' the young male said in genuine admiration. 'You're well filled out and sturdyish. Your coat's a picture. You've got strong shoulders and feet. You'll be a mighty hunter and fighter one day. And you've your mother to thank for your healthy looks.'

Moja was puzzled afresh. He didn't know what to make of this lion who seemed a bully one minute and a friendly older brother the next. Challenger sensibly took Moja to the nearest sheltered pool where, undisturbed, the cub was able to cool his thirst. Challenger drank next to him, keeping a watch for unwanted intruders all the while. Afterwards the lion made haste to lead the cub back to his den.

'My turn to be hungry,' Challenger announced bluntly. 'I need to catch something for myself.' He expected Moja to take the hint and hide himself obediently in the rocks.

But the cub said, 'I'll come with you.'

'Out of the question!' Challenger snapped. 'I can't have you getting in the way when I'm stalking.'

'I don't get in the way,' Moja asserted indignantly. 'I'm used to following the adults when they hunt. All the cubs do. We're not babies any more.'

Challenger was adamant. 'You'll stay here,' he insisted. 'I want no distractions. Now, go on. Do as I say.'

Moja knew it was pointless to argue. He took himself back into the rocks but had already decided he would follow Challenger without the adult's knowledge.

'As soon as he's far enough away not to notice,' Moja vowed to himself, 'I'll go after him. I want some real meat. I bet he won't be catching those green things for his own meal.'

3

Uneasy Companions

Once Challenger's back was turned Moja edged out of the hole and watched to see which direction the older male would take. Challenger strode ahead purposefully. He had no reason to suspect that Moja would disobey him. He didn't turn his head but broke into a swinging trot as he picked out his prey.

A mother gnu and her calf had distanced themselves from the main herd. The mother was completely absorbed in some choice new shoots of pasture in the wide green expanse of the plains and hadn't noticed that the rest of the group had moved further off. The calf stuck by her side and Challenger's steady, determined gaze focused itself on the little creature as he approached the pair. A pack of hunting dogs with their patchwork black, white and yellow coats, long legs and big erect ears were loitering nearby. Their hungry mouths gaped and drooled as they sized up their chances of intercepting the young lion and taking the calf from under his nose. Challenger knew they were there and that they were competitors. As he neared the unsuspecting mother and calf he slowed and dropped down to a stalking posture. Although he didn't for a moment lose sight of his target he was also keeping an eye on the dogs, who were milling about as though waiting for their leader to make a dart. Moja, slinking forward in Challenger's wake, watched these competitors excitedly. He looked from them to the young lion and back again, thrilled to be a witness of this drama of rivalry. The dogs were aware of Moja too. An unprotected lion cub was a secondary target if the first one should prove unattainable.

Suddenly Challenger made his move. He had no choice. The dogs had sprung forward on impulse and the lion bounded across the uneven ground to head them off. At last the mother gnu realised her predicament. She began to run, her calf keeping level, but the pair had left flight too late. Challenger raced up and, with one hefty blow, knocked the calf sprawling on its back. The lion made sure of his prey, grabbing it by the throat and turning to face the rush of the dogs. The pack slid to a halt, yapping in frustration and trying to assess, even now, whether there was a chance they could rob the lion of his kill. Challenger dropped the dead calf and bared his teeth in a ferocious snarl, whipping out his claws and raking the air in an unmistakable warning. The dogs veered away, deciding the risk was greater than they were prepared to take. And now they sought compensation, loping swiftly round to where Moja was vainly trying to hide behind a decaying tree-stump.

Challenger began his meal but still kept one eye on the hunting dogs, whose behaviour he knew from experience was unpredictable. He saw the lion cub for the first time as Moja jumped up and began to run from his pursuers. His squeals for help were urgent, yet Challenger hesitated, loath to abandon a meal which could easily be stolen in his absence. However, he was unable to continue eating in comfort while he watched the dogs homing in for their own kill. In the long run Moja's value to him was paramount. Challenger left the carcass and gave chase himself, roaring with all the bluster of which a healthy male lion is capable. As he did so, he realised he wanted to rescue Moja for another reason, too. The cub was one of his own kind, after all, and he didn't want to see him being savaged by a pack of dogs.

The hunters were intimidated by Challenger's charge, but only for a moment. They knew they could outrun him. And they were clever. Relinquishing the substitute prey they wheeled round, quickly aware that the dead gnu calf was now theirs for the taking. As Challenger panted to a stop by the frightened lion cub the leading dog snatched up the carcass by its head and started to drag it away. The other members of the pack snapped at the body until it was dropped and all the dogs lunged at it together, grabbing what mouthfuls they could.

'You stupid little creature!' Challenger roared at Moja. 'Where did you think you were going?'

'I . . . I . . .' stammered Moja.

'To your death, that's where you were going,' Challenger bellowed furiously. 'What if I hadn't been here?' He spun round. 'Look what you've done!' he spluttered. 'You've lost me my kill! Those dogs'll '
He broke off, growling, and made a half-hearted run towards the pack. But he knew it was useless. They were easily able to evade him, gulping at their shares of the meat while they ran.

Moja was dejected and very contrite. He turned and trudged back to Challenger's boulder, his head sunk low between his forelegs. Challenger caught him up. 'Don't ever do that again,' he admonished him. 'You see what happens when you try to go it alone? You're too young and too tender to go unprotected. You nearly made those dogs a nice little meal. I hope you've learnt a lesson.'

'Yes,' Moja whispered. 'And I'm sorry you've had to go hungry. I'm really grateful to you for – for saving me.'

Challenger relented. 'All right,' he said with more sympathy. 'You've had a bad scare. So it evens out in a way, doesn't it?'

'Shall I go into hiding again?' Moja asked humbly.

'Yes. I have to satisfy my hunger somehow. There might be some scraps remaining from my stolen meal.' Now Challenger sounded angry again.

'There's some of the meat you brought me. I haven't eaten all of it. If – if you'd like it,' Moja offered uncertainly.

'Lizard? I don't think so. Keep it!' Challenger growled.

Moja could think of nothing else to make amends. 'I know I did a stupid thing and I've made you really angry,' he murmured, 'but – but – you will still help me to find my pride?'

Challenger considered for a moment. He had no intention of abandoning his plan and he thought how he could best turn Moja's misdemeanour to his advantage. 'You will have to do *exactly* as I say from now on,' he told the cub briskly. 'No matter what happens. Is that understood?'

'Yes, Challenger.'

'Then it's settled. That's our pact.'

During the next couple of days Moja's pride moved further off. The lions were following the herds of prey as the latter continually sought fresh pasture. Challenger managed to keep them in view but he found himself travelling increasingly longer distances from his den area. If it hadn't been for Moja and the need to keep him fed and under observation, the young male would have deserted his usual base.

Huru and Kimya, the sister lionesses, were the hunters for the pride. Their skill and intuition meant that their hunting resulted in a high proportion of kills. All the pride members ate well. The big males Battlescars and Blackmane sometimes collaborated in a hunt, although whether they did or didn't made no difference to the rule that they always fed first and took the best of the meat. The lionesses came second and the cubs were tolerated as they tried to seize what bits they could so long as they didn't overstep the mark. The system worked well in the wet season whilst prey was abundant on the plains.

Challenger was cautious in his approach. Huru and Kimya had no idea they were being tracked. It was the males' job to watch for intruders and Battlescars and his brother were perfectly aware of Challenger's presence. They remembered him but made no move while he kept his distance. Yet the young adult's vigil was irksome.

'We should leave here,' Battlescars said as they lay panting in the heat of the day. 'We need to look after our other interests.'

'You're right,' his brother agreed. 'And as soon as we do, our constant young shadow's waiting game will be over.'

'He'll be around the sisters the moment we're out of sight.'

'We could set a trap for him,' Blackmane growled.

'I've been thinking the same thing,' Battlescars said.

Moja began to doubt Challenger's motives. Every time he asked the young adult about returning to his pride he got the same answer.

'Not just yet. It's not safe enough.'

The first time he was told this Moja reminded Challenger that he had said it would have to be at dusk.

'It will be,' Challenger had responded. 'Darkness is the only possible time for you to travel in safety. But we must choose an occasion when there will be the least interference.'

After that Moja's question was repeated regularly and always met with the same response. The lion cub was tired of remaining in the same confined area, either hidden away in the rock hole he had come to hate or crouching nearby to eat what was brought him or to lap from a pool. Because of the distance he had to cover, Challenger's absences became more protracted. Moja was half inclined to run away, but the pact he had made with Challenger kept him rooted to the spot. His only hope was that eventually his unwanted guardian would decide it was safe enough for him to be taken to rejoin his pride, although as time passed his faith in this outcome was gradually being eroded.

The day came when Challenger couldn't find Moja's pride at all. Moving with care as usual he scanned what he understood to be Huru and Kimya's territory without so much as a glimpse of them. Panting with exasperation, he slunk to a much-used waterhole which he knew the entire pride visited on occasion. An area of bush fringed one end of the pool. Challenger lay down to wait. He didn't venture into the thicker vegetation straight away but positioned himself under cover at its edge where his tawny hide was well screened. Without stirring he watched successive groups of animals come to drink, from zebra to antelope to a mother rhino and her calf. But no lion showed up. Finally he went to drink himself, keeping constant watch as he did so. He was on the point of leaving when all at once the sister lionesses with their remaining cubs arrived at the waterside. Their appearance was by then so unexpected and sudden that Challenger was startled. Anticipating that Battlescars and Blackmane would now soon appear on the scene, he hastened to return to cover. The sisters' faces were red with gore and so were those of the cubs. They had recently feasted and were thirsty. Challenger recalled his own empty stomach but he dared not move again yet.

Kimya had spotted his retreat from the pool and stood for a long while looking towards his hiding-place. She thought she saw him still lurking amongst some foliage. The dipping sun was reflected in the water, making everything shimmer in a golden haze. She couldn't be sure, but she was eager to know his identity. She remembered how she had persuaded Blackmane to spare a young male who had been badly beaten in a fight.

'Yes, he was a daring youngster. Foolish, too,' she murmured to herself. 'I wondered if we'd see him again.'

Huru noticed her abstraction. 'What is it, sister?'

'Look. Over there. D'you recall the courageous young male?'

'The stout one with all the bravado? Of course. Is that him?'

'I'm fairly certain of it,' said Kimya. 'And if it is him, he's here because of us.'

Huru looked solemn. Her first thought was for her young. 'We should move away,' she advised. 'And get the cubs into cover. Battlescars is absent. We can't take chances, whoever that young lion is.'

Kimya didn't respond at once, but bent her head to lap some more. The cubs were splashing in and out of the pool, reckless of any danger as they played.

'Come on, sister,' Huru urged her. 'It's not safe here. We both know what a determined male is capable of.'

'Wouldn't you like to be sure who it is who's so interested in us?' Kimya asked artlessly.

'We'll find out soon enough,' Huru growled, and began to move off. She nudged Mbili and Tatu, calling them away from their games. The other cubs followed instinctively and finally Kimya turned and, with a final long glance at the half-hidden male, brought up the rear.

Challenger remained where he was for a while, still expecting Battlescars and Blackmane to show up. But as time went on he at last began to suspect that, quite by chance, he had discovered the lionesses alone. He pulled himself from his screen and padded, cautiously as always, after them. He paced alongside the pool, his eyes raking the more open country beyond for sight of the two proud sisters he so much admired.

And there they were with their cubs running between them, just breasting the last of a patch of scrub. Challenger checked his immediate surroundings, then broke into a trot. Almost as he did so he heard the first roars of the males who had tricked him. Crashing through the undergrowth skirting the pool, Battlescars and Blackmane leapt on the astonished Challenger from behind, their claws and teeth digging deep into his hide. A din of roaring from all three lions made Huru and Kimya pause and look back. They saw Challenger on his back, fighting furiously for survival, kicking out viciously with his feet at the exposed undersides of his assailants. Blackmane was torn and lost his grip on the younger lion, but Battlescars continued to deal savage bites on his opponent. He aimed a lunge at the throat area which would have been fatal had it connected. But Challenger twisted free and battled hard, knowing his life was at stake. The lionesses hurried away, driving the cubs before them, and were soon out of sight.

Gasping in agony, Blackmane limped off to tend his wounds. He was badly ripped; blood flowed from several gashes along his chest and belly. With him out of the picture Challenger and Battlescars fought a straightforward contest for supremacy, and eventually Battlescars's greater strength and experience began to tell. The younger lion's resistance wavered until finally, severely mauled, he managed to wriggle clear and stagger away. Completely exhausted, Battlescars was incapable of following up his advantage by pursuing Challenger and killing him. He stood on quivering legs, heaving great lungfuls of air, his eyes so dulled by his exertions that he could scarcely make out the direction of Challenger's retreat.

When he had recovered his breath, he moved unsteadily towards his brother and slumped alongside him. 'The youngster's beaten,' he murmured.

'But at what cost?' Blackmane croaked. 'Look at me. Now you must travel on alone.'

'Never!' Battlescars declared. 'I'll wait for you to recover, brother. How could I leave you?'

'You must,' Blackmane insisted hoarsely. 'I shall never move from here. I've no strength left.'

With a heavy heart, Battlescars acknowledged the truth of his brother's words. Blackmane's wounds were terrible; Challenger had dealt him his death blow. 'I shall stay with you none the less,' he said compassionately. 'Until . . .'

'Until I tell you to go,' Blackmane forced himself to say. 'And I do tell you. Go, brother. Find our other pride and see that all's well. I ask for nothing else.'

Battlescars sighed. 'So be it,' he replied sadly.

Challenger, meanwhile, had disappeared. The young lion had reached the shelter of the bush at the edge of the waterhole and collapsed. There was no

way he could get back to his old den and he thought
of Moja, isolated and now unprotected, waiting in
vain for his return.

4

Battleground

The warden of the game park, Simon Obagwe, and his little daughter Annie had been witnesses when a cow elephant had found Moja too close to her dead calf and had slung him out of the way. It had upset Annie greatly and she never ceased to wonder what had happened to the cub. From the beginning the little girl had been involved in the lives of Huru and Kimya, when the lionesses had been in the care of her father Simon at Kamenza. She had been thrilled when cubs had been born to the sisters and Moja's fate concerned her greatly. She pestered her father for news each time he returned from his rounds. His reply was always the same. 'No, Annie. There's no sign of him.' He wouldn't tell her the cub was dead because he didn't know if that was the truth. Yet of course he suspected it was.

'Have you asked Joel if he's seen him?' Annie would then ask. Joel, who had once been Huru's and Kimya's keeper in the English zoo, was now assistant manager of the Kamenza animal refuge centre. When time permitted he liked to take a Land-Rover into the game park, sometimes on his own, to look for the sister lionesses and their pride.

'I don't need to ask him,' Simon would tell his daughter. 'You know he would tell me at once.'

Annie's disappointment never seemed to lessen with each repetition. She believed Moja was alive, but even she realised that if he didn't soon reappear it would mean he had been unable to survive on his own.

And now his survival really did look uncertain. When Challenger failed to appear Moja remained for a time out of sight in the hole in the rocks. He kept a constant check on the outside, staring from the entrance for any sign of his strange companion. When night fell and he was still alone, Moja recalled what Challenger had said about darkness being the only safe time for him to move.

He was worried about the young adult. Challenger was the key to his rejoining his pride. Without the older lion he had little hope of finding it. Furthermore, Challenger had brought his food. Now Moja was very hungry and it seemed there was no prospect of being fed. He pattered about by Challenger's boulder, listening to every slight sound for a hint of the noise of a lion. Bird calls, hyenas' cries, jackals' yaps and, once, the snarl of a leopard were all that came to his ears. The big cat's cry was close. Moja shrank back against the rocks, his heart fluttering nervously. He yearned for the security of the pride: his mother's reassuring presence, his father's haughty stare, even the playful bickering of his siblings. He knew the likelihood now was that he would have to search for them alone. But there was one other possibility. If he could find Challenger first, perhaps the young male could still lend assistance in some way. Moja screwed up his courage and waited for the leopard to pass. He saw its stealthy figure slink through the shadows only two or three metres away, half turning its head as it caught his scent. It moved on and Moja recovered his breath.

'I can't stay here,' he whispered to himself. 'I'll go quietly and carefully and follow Challenger's direction. I know which way he used to go.' He waited a sensible interval longer so as not to run any risk of colliding with the leopard, then paced forward. Cool air blew against his face. It smelt clean and sweet after the stale smells he had endured in the rocky cleft. Hunger nagged at him insistently. His hunter's instinct was alert for the slightest chance of a kill; there was always the possibility that one of the many small nocturnal rodents would cross his path. And he tried to talk himself out of his fearfulness. 'I'm Battlescars's son,' he chanted as a constant reminder. 'I can look after myself.'

He reached the place where the hunting dogs had cornered him and here he made his first kill. A grass rat, garnering seeds for its larder, was an easy target for an agile lion cub. He crunched the rodent with relish and his success encouraged him tremendously. He felt a new sense of independence and began to think about how he could best pursue his search for Challenger.

'Darkness may be safer,' Moja murmured to himself, 'but it's no help when you're looking for something.' He decided to spend the night hours hunting, then find a place to lie up as dawn approached. Then in the daylight he could judge for himself whether there was a chance of beginning a search.

Small prey, Moja found, was easy to come by. He was able to satisfy his appetite and to practise his own method of hunting. By dawn all the running, jumping and pouncing had tired him out. He climbed into the fork of an acacia, not far off the ground, and fell asleep.

Daylight woke Challenger, who hadn't moved from his hiding-place for the best part of a day. His morale was at a low ebb. Vanquished again by Battlescars, he had lost all confidence in his ability to compete for a mate. He no longer felt like a challenger. He was weak from loss of blood, gashed and torn in a dozen places, and had a raging thirst. When he tried to heave himself to his feet his trembling limbs protested at his body's weight and he collapsed on to his side. But water was maddeningly close and he made another attempt to rise. Half crawling, half pulling himself along on his belly, the young lion managed to reach the near edge of the pool. His body subsided into the water and he lay where he was for several minutes, perfectly still. Sunshine skipped over the surface of the pool. Warmth and the refreshing feel of the water revived him, and gradually he became aware of his senses returning. He roused and lapped greedily. Then he struggled to his feet and stood with the water up to his chin. The sound of racking breaths and long drawn out groans came to his ears. He turned and there was Blackmane at the other end of the pool, staggering and sliding into the water just as he had done. Challenger had forgotten Blackmane.

The sight of the older lion in as bad a plight as he put new heart into him. He remembered how he had forced Blackmane out of the fight and suddenly all his old spirit rekindled. Yes, he had been defeated. But it had needed two lions to do it: big, powerful animals who had fought and conquered across wide swaths of territory. And now he, Challenger, had laid one of them low. Blackmane was out of the running for good. Challenger watched the older animal, who was indeed in a parlous state. Flaps of flesh hung loose on his underside as though they had been peeled back. Challenger crept forward, ready to gloat.

'You've done for me,' Blackmane muttered hoarsely. 'I shall never heal.'

Challenger saw the water red where Blackmane was sprawled. A shred of sympathy checked his feeling of triumph. This lion's period of supremacy was over and there was nothing left for him but a few lingering invalid days as he waited for death to claim him. Then Challenger recalled the ambush and his sympathy vanished.

'You and your brother plotted to finish me,' he said. 'It didn't quite work out, did it? I'm not finished after all. I shall lie low for a while and recover my strength. There'll be another chance for me.'

Blackmane listened and knew he was right. One day it would be Challenger's time to dominate. There was nothing more to say. It was the pattern of things.

The lions parted, Challenger to go to his hiding-place in the bush, Blackmane to await the return of his brother. For the first time Battlescars had had to travel alone to their other pride in the north. Blackmane dreaded that he would be driven from it by rivals. The days when the brothers had held three prides were well and truly over. Now even two prides might well prove too much for one ageing male.

Moja welcomed the sunlight. He felt strong and wasn't afraid. He climbed higher up the acacia and balanced himself to get a view through the branches. He saw zebra with their barrel chests and long legs feeding amongst the dew. There was no familiar tawny shape of a lion in evidence. The morning was quiet. Then, suddenly, Moja realised there was another animal in the tree. Whatever it was, it was asleep. Its rasping

snore, peaceful and regular had roused Moja's curiosity. He looked about him and what he saw nearly
made him drop to the ground. A fully grown leopard
with matchless camouflage dozed in the midst of the
sun-dappled branches, its limbs dangling lazily from
its perch and its noble face twitching as it enjoyed
dreams of hunting. Moja felt certain it was the same
beast that had passed close by him the previous night.
He was enthralled by this picture of latent power,
but he didn't loiter too long in his admiration. He
clambered to the trunk of the tree and, digging in
hard with his claws, reversed down to the ground.
Making the most of the quiet, he set off at a trot,
keeping under cover as much as he could.

Chance brought Moja to the very pool where his
father and uncle had fought for their lives. Signs of a
battle were not difficult to detect: tufts of mane, spilt
blood and mingled scents of lion made Moja shiver
in anticipation. He recognised Battlescars's scent at
once, and looked all round for his father. Where was
he? Then he saw the big black-maned male lying half
in and half out of the water. Already vultures were
circling nearby. Moja rushed to the prone animal's
side. The lion was dying. Moja saw it was Blackmane.
He stared at the fallen giant, unsure how to react.
When he sniffed at his uncle, Blackmane's dull eyes
fixed on him and a gasp escaped from his open
mouth. He didn't recognise Moja.

'Is my father here?' the cub whispered.

There was no reply. Blackmane's life was over.

Not understanding, Moja tried to stir him. 'Blackmane? Blackmane! Where's my father? Can't you tell
me? Oh, poor creature. Poor lion.' He knew something awful had happened. Where was Battlescars?
The two big males were usually seen together. And

where was the rest of the pride? Moja was more desperate than ever to find out.

A voice called him, but not one from his own family. It was Challenger, who had seen him nuzzling Blackmane and recognised his perplexity. 'Over here, cub. Over here.'

Moja traced the voice and found his recent companion in almost the same miserable state as Blackmane. He was shocked and scared. 'What . . . what . . .' he stammered.

'I was ambushed,' Challenger told him. 'Two males against one. We fought. I was nearly killed. But I survived. One of my enemies didn't.'

Moja gaped. He glanced at his uncle's body, then back at Challenger. 'You . . . you did that?' he gasped.

'I fought for my life,' Challenger growled.

'But . . . where is Battlescars? Where is my father?' Moja demanded.

'Him? Oh, he sloped off eventually. I made sure he carried a few more scars too,' Challenger finished boastfully.

Moja backed away. How could he ever have trusted this animal? Challenger would never have led him back to the pride he regarded as his enemies. Moja did not yet understand that the pride females were far from enemies in Challenger's eyes. He turned and scampered away without pausing for a moment by the still body of Blackmane. His priority now was to find the rest of his family. Too battered to prevent him, Challenger watched as the cub he had planned to use to lure Huru from her pride vanished from sight.

The rest of the pride knew nothing of Blackmane's death. After Huru and Kimya had taken the cubs away they had seen no more of the males. They believed that Battlescars and Blackmane must now be renewing control of their other pride to the north. Defeat for either of the brothers was something the lionesses didn't contemplate. Now they were lying on a soft mat of grass a considerable distance from the pool, their cubs mostly asleep, lolling against their legs and sides. The sisters had some curiosity about that other pride whose attention claimed periodic visits from the males.

'Do you ever feel relief,' Kimya asked as she gave Sita a comforting lick, 'when our mates leave us for a spell?'

'No,' Huru answered. 'I prefer them to be with us. More protection that way.'

'You're thinking of the young male, the brave one?' Kimya asked.

'Yes. Was he *so* brave, though?' Huru queried. 'He had two brothers with him when he first came snooping.'

'They're not around now,' Kimya said dismissively, and yawned. 'And even Battlescars was impressed by that young upstart.'

'It's clear you are as well,' Huru remarked gruffly. 'I hope your allegiance isn't wavering. Blackmane is the father of your cubs.'

'Of course I'm not wavering, sister. Blackmane and Battlescars are the finest males around. But they are ageing.'

Huru couldn't dispute this and she did wonder if one day the brothers' reign might come to an end. She watched Mbili and Tatu sleeping with their heads resting on one another and felt an overwhelming tenderness. Then she looked away and into the distance. Moja came into her mind again: her firstborn cub still missing in this wilderness. She ached to know what had happened to him. But she pushed the

thought away. She had learnt that it was of no value
to dwell on it.

Every night, after his last encounter with Challenger,
Moja was crossing country that unfortunately took
him farther away from his pride on each successive
journey. He had nothing and no one to guide him
and was actually wandering haphazardly, following the
same programme of catching small nocturnal prey
as he travelled, then finding a hideaway at dawn.
Sometimes he continued his search by daylight hours
if the landscape seemed quiet and empty. Eventually
he began to hear lion calls and he tried to track them,
listening hard for a roar he would recognise.

One night the calls seemed very close and Moja was
absolutely certain he could hear his father's voice.
Those earthshaking roars of possession were too familiar to mistake. Moja thrilled to the sound, which set
the air all around vibrating. Answering roars from
other males followed. Moja knew then that his father
had competition. Without knowing it the cub had
brought himself close to his father's other, bigger
pride rather than to his own. But he did know that
Battlescars was alone now and had no Blackmane to
support him. He was excited but anxious. He remembered that Challenger had already dealt his father
some wounding blows, perhaps weakening him. Moja
none the less believed Battlescars to be invincible. He
had never known him to be beaten. He settled down
in a disused hare's burrow and listened to the
exchange of taunts and claims.

On that night the calls led to nothing. Battlescars
seemed so close that Moja determined to reach him
the next day. He was tired of being on his own. He
had been fortunate so far in avoiding danger, but he
needed the reassuring companionship of an adult. At

dawn he found a useful look-out point in the shape of a weatherbeaten termite mound. From its crumbling crest Moja saw a gathering of lionesses with their young. Cubs of his age and others much older were in evidence. He was sure this was his father's pride and he sighed with relief. He pictured Battlescars's surprise and welcome when he greeted him and he waited impatiently for him to emerge.

As the daylight strengthened Moja noticed three males half hidden in some longer grass but close enough to the females to suggest they were bonded. The cub was puzzled. Was one of these his father? He had to find out.

He clambered from his mound and padded forward anxiously, wondering if he should call out to Battlescars. But there was no time to decide. Five females and some of the older cubs confronted him within moments with snarls and threatening faces.

'What are you doing here?'

'Whose cub are you?'

Their demanding voices held menace.

'I'm Battlescars's cub,' Moja answered stoutly, expecting them to change their attitude to him immediately. But their antagonism remained.

'His day's over,' snarled one of the younger females. 'And so is yours, young cub. You made a big mistake coming here.'

'But I – I *heard* him,' Moja insisted. 'I heard his voice. He can't just have *gone* like that.'

'He's gone all right,' another growled. 'Didn't even put up a fight when he saw how he was outnumbered.'

Moja glanced towards where the three males were beginning to stir themselves to investigate him and he realised the truth. He had blundered into an alien pride that was completely hostile to him.

—5—

Joel

Moja's only hope was to run. He guessed the males would kill him if they got the chance; a few fleeting seconds and all would be over. He looked round for a patch of cover as the lions circled. There was none. He could think only of the termite mound where he had watched for his father. There was nothing else within reach that offered any kind of sanctuary.

As Moja started to run one of the males let out a roar that so terrified him that it lent wings to his feet. He flew towards the earthen pillar with the males in hot pursuit. The cub's lead was scanty. The lions' longer strides brought them within a metre of his rear as, instinctively, he dived into an underground chamber at the base of the mound. There was barely room for him to pull himself clear of his pursuers. Dust and grit showered down on him and clogged his nostrils. But the ancient excavations of the insect hordes who had once lived in and developed this extraordinary structure were Moja's salvation now. He panted, half choking, as he breathed in more debris. The males grumbled and snarled outside. Moja flinched at each sound, his body rigid with the expectation that powerful claws would soon rip through his shield and tug him clear. Where was his father now that he needed a parent's protection? Moja couldn't believe that Battlescars had tamely given up his reign to these lions without more than a few token roars. Perhaps he was still nearby, plotting his next move. Moja was heartened by the idea and refused to accept what he had been told. In the meantime all he could do was to lie still and wait. There wasn't enough space even to wriggle.

He heard the lions discussing him. One was eager to kill him. 'Any cub of Battlescars should be disposed of.' Moja heard and shuddered. The others were half-hearted about it. A rainstorm had begun and seemed to be cooling their tempers.

Moja lay huddled on the earth floor of the partly collapsed insect fortress and listened to the heavy drumming of raindrops above and around him. The storm's strength increased by degrees so that soon the sound of torrential rain was all he could hear. As the moments passed he felt a little more secure but he didn't dare to hope that the lions had dispersed.

The storm lasted a long time. When it finally eased Moja was cold, damp and muddy but still at liberty. The group of lions had deserted his refuge and he was free to leave. He backed out of the chamber, sneezed and shook his coat free of debris. A strong wind from the north had whisked the black clouds away and the land steamed as the sun reasserted itself.

Moja's one thought was to track his father, but he had no way of knowing how to do it. He only knew that if he could catch up with Battlescars, the old male would lead him back to his family. Moja sniffed for clues. He smelt what he hoped was his father's scent but it was so mixed up with the dominant scents of the three male usurpers that it was difficult to be sure. In any case the cub had no choice but to travel in a direction that took him away from the hostile pride. And as quickly as possible.

He set off in the direction he believed he detected Battlescars's scent. 'Wait for me, Father,' he whispered. 'If only you'd wait for me.'

After the rain, a dejected and morose Battlescars stepped from a thorn thicket in which he had dozed through the downpour. His proud and disdainful expression was gone now. Without his brother Blackmane's support his supremacy was undermined. Faced with the prospect of further fighting such a short time after the terrible battle with Challenger, Battlescars's resolve had weakened and he had settled for the easy way out. He had succumbed to the younger males' threat, turned tail, and plodded away. He still held the small pride to the south, and was willing to be content with that. His territory and power diminished, Battlescars knew that one day he would be cast out altogether. Old would give way to new; age and experience to youth and muscle. His head held low against the glare and the heat, the once mighty dark-maned male comforted himself with the knowledge that Huru and Kimya would be sure to accept him back despite his reduced status. He had no heart to take the news of his humiliation to Blackmane. He believed his brother was dead; if not, he was almost certainly beyond help, and Battlescars grieved that he could take him no comfort. Instead, he headed straight for his remaining pride.

A Land-Rover from Kamenza bounced through mud and puddles fifty metres from the solitary lion. Joel, the assistant manager of the refuge centre, was looking once again for his precious lionesses and their cubs. He noticed new, major wounds on the old fighter's sides, and followed him slowly and at a distance, stopping every so often to use his binoculars. Battlescars ignored the faint throb of the vehicle's engine.

He had long ago become accustomed to such noises. Joel nodded to himself with a wry smile as he watched Battlescars's unwavering gait. Then he swung his glasses round in a wide arc, trying to pinpoint Huru and Kimya. He didn't see them, but what he did see made him give an exclamation.

'Well! Who can that be?' He studied what appeared to be a lion cub, trotting confidently through some short grasses as if it knew exactly where it was going. Joel was excited. He dared not hope for too much. It could be any cub, after all; perhaps one temporarily separated from a larger group. If only he could get closer! He studied the terrain. It was fairly open; patches of scrub were easily avoidable. He put down his glasses and took the steering wheel again. Moving slowly and circumspectly, Joel managed to close the gap between himself and the cub. But the youngster detected the engine noise and showed alarm. As it turned its head slightly to check on the vehicle Joel let out a cry. He had recognised Moja.

'So it *is* you! Alive and well too. Terrific! But why are you going *that* way? Your father isn't. And where's the rest of the pride?'

Joel was puzzled, and rightly so, because Moja, without realising it, was once more travelling in the opposite direction from the one he needed if he wanted to find Battlescars. Joel continued to follow at a discreet distance. He wanted to know where Moja was heading so that he could find him again. Already he could picture Annie's joy at hearing the news. He was sure Simon would have no peace after that until he had taken his daughter to see the stray cub for herself. But Joel wasn't happy about Moja's apparently aimless direction.

'Where is he heading?' he muttered as the cub veered off on another path. 'I don't think he knows.

Surely he hasn't been wandering about like this all along, unable to find his family?' It did seem possible and Joel considered whether it was ethical to intervene. In the game park Nature had to have a free hand, yet Joel felt himself to be so intimately bound up with the lives of Huru and Kimya that he had a particular sympathy for the poor lost cub. He wrestled with the problem, continuing to follow cautiously but at the same time as closely as he dared.

It was the worst thing he could have done. Moja knew the vehicle was following him and it made him nervous. He had been well protected from the sight of humans and their vehicles at close quarters. His mother had seen to that as he and her other cubs grew up. The noise of a car engine to a lion's keen hearing was unsettling. Now Moja lost all track of his intentions in his effort to get away from it. He forgot about his father and his attempt to join him. He tried running one way, then another, but nothing seemed to shake the Land-Rover off. Then he panicked. He was still just a cub, after all, and Joel realised too late that he was the cause of Moja's strange behaviour. By then Moja was bounding blindly towards a wide and fast-flowing river.

Joel stopped the vehicle at once and turned off the engine, cursing himself for his stupidity. 'What on earth was I thinking of?' he cried aloud. 'Whatever's going to happen now?'

He lost sight of Moja and jumped out of the car. 'He's heading for big trouble that way,' he told himself, 'and I've caused it. So I've got to help now if I can, whether I like it or not.' He abandoned the Land-Rover and plunged ahead on foot. Picking his way through the shorter grasses, he made the best speed he could.

Moja was running scared and attracting attention.

There were hyenas about and, nearer the river, the pack of hunting dogs that had stolen Challenger's kill. A young unprotected animal, even a lion, and running free like Moja, was bound to be of interest to predators. The cub was in mortal danger and Joel was powerless to help. He saw the hyenas swing into a loping chase ahead and, although he couldn't now see Moja, he guessed what they were after. The hunting dogs kept their distance this time. A pack of hyenas was just about the most tenacious of all the game park's predators and was to be avoided. But another hunter, a solitary one, was lying drowsing on a branch of a commiphora tree overhanging the river and was right in Moja's path.

The cub was approaching the water. He heard the hyenas' cries and his fright was the only thing that kept his tired lungs and legs going flat out. He spied the commiphora tree with its twisted branches and knew it was his best chance of escape. He had just enough breath and strength to leap upwards to safety before the hyena pack came milling around the tree's base, whooping their shrill eerie cries. On a higher branch the lone hunter – a female leopard – awoke with a start. She saw the gasping lion cub at once and bared her teeth in a warning, her spotted face full of fury. Hyenas were her enemy, often stealing her kills, and now Moja had brought a pack of them to her roost. Her lithe, muscular body bunched together as tense as a coiled spring and her long tail flailed angrily. She snarled at Moja and lashed out with one paw. The cub gathered himself to jump clear. Between the hyenas on the ground and the leopard in the tree he saw the river not as a barrier but as his sole escape route. He leapt outwards and landed in an awkward heap on the bank. Quickly recovering himself, he half slid and half sprang into the water. The current caught him and bundled him along, carrying him from the place of danger but threatening to submerge him.

Moja fought to keep his head above water as he was carried out from the bank towards midstream. His weary legs paddled in vain, making no impression on the direction the river wanted to take him. However, there was slacker water ahead and he finally came to rest against what he thought was a large rock. The cub's inert body, washed to and fro by the ripples, bumped gently against this obstruction while he gasped for breath. Suddenly the object reared up, revealing the massive head and body of a hippo who had been contentedly wallowing in the shallow water close to the bank. Moja found himself on its leathery back. He hastily scrambled clear and ended up on the opposite side of the river from where he had begun.

For a while, completely exhausted, he simply lay still. He knew without having to think about it that he was farther away from his family than ever. Somehow he had crossed this moving water and if he was ever to rejoin his pride he had to find a way of crossing back again.

—6—

Mother and Calf

Joel returned to his vehicle very downhearted. He hadn't seen Moja again. It had been too dangerous to approach the hyenas and he could only calculate the most likely outcome of events. He didn't believe Moja could have escaped the pack and he bitterly regretted his own part in what he feared was the youngster's death. How quickly his joy of discovering the lion cub had given way to gloom and despondency. Now he had to relate the sad tale to his superior, Simon Obagwe.

'I'll swear him to secrecy as far as poor Annie is concerned,' Joel decided. 'She mustn't know about this.'

Back at Kamenza his gloomy face brought immediate questions from Simon. Joel described what had happened. Simon remained quiet while he listened, nodding occasionally.

'I see,' he said afterwards. 'Well, you shouldn't blame yourself. And in any case you don't know for sure if the cub is dead.' He put a hand on Joel's shoulder. 'Time will tell. Until then . . .'

Joel began, 'Annie—'

'I know,' Simon said. 'Not a word.'

*

When Moja had recovered a little from his ordeal, he knew the first thing he needed to do was to get under cover somewhere. After a succession of alarms and dangers all he wanted was a period of quiet while he took stock of his situation. He was farther from home than ever and he didn't know what perils might be lurking on this side of the water. He was very, very tired and he got to his feet to look for a place to rest. He was wary of trees now and he remembered the hole in the rocks by Challenger's boulder. Somewhere as secure as that, no matter how smelly, was what he wanted.

He went slowly along the bank. There was a sort of rocky point, he discovered, that overhung the river. He thought there should be a hole in or around it somewhere that he could squeeze himself into. And there was; in fact there were several. So Moja was able to reject the foulest ones, which reeked of other creatures' droppings, and to choose one that was a little sweeter. He lay down and, with a grateful sigh, fell fast asleep.

It was dark when he awoke. He had slept a long time and he felt a lot better, apart from being ravenously hungry. He hadn't far to go to solve that problem. A scrabbling noise in one of the rock crevices drew him quickly from his den. Moments later he had killed the scrabbler – a mongoose – and was devouring it safely in his refuge.

Moja was content to lie low. He felt stronger and he was growing in confidence after emerging from his spate of adventures unharmed. But he didn't relish facing any more difficulties for a while and he simply had no idea how he was going to meet the challenge of crossing the river. He slept again until thirst eventually drove him back to the water's edge. After drinking deeply he stood watching the flow. At that point it was comparatively sluggish, but Moja was unable to recognise this. All he could remember was how he had been swept along once he had dropped into it, and he didn't wish to repeat the experience.

'I may have to stay on this side,' Moja thought to himself. How lonely that made him feel. 'No. No, that's impossible,' he decided. 'There must be something or somebody who can help.'

It wasn't so easy looking for help, though. Moja's only friends were the members of his own pride. Even Challenger had turned out to be an adversary and anyway he, like Moja's family, was on the wrong side of the river. Moja returned once more to his refuge and lay there, feeling increasingly miserable. He longed for companionship, yet he knew there was an almost insurmountable barrier to his finding it again. Sleep claimed him once more. The next time he awoke he heard, close by, animal sounds in the river.

It was light again. Moja emerged from his den and crept to the nearer side of the promontory. He saw an adult black rhinoceros slurping water from the river as she stood up to her neck in the current with every appearance of enjoyment. A rhino calf was lying in a patch of mud closer inshore, apparently oblivious of the fact that a pair of oxpecker birds were using him as a dining-table. They were jabbing their beaks into folds in his skin and even around his mouth and nostrils in their search for ticks and insects. The calf seemed to be having a snooze. Moja crept closer. He felt there was no threat here. But as he did so the mother rhino gave a snort and turned her head towards him. Her little short-sighted eyes tried to focus as she sniffed the air. She was always wary of the smell of lion. Moja paused, making the rhino unable to distinguish his small body from its surroundings.

'Where are you, lion?' she snuffled. 'Don't come any closer.'

The calf awoke and struggled to his feet. Moja was closer to him than the adult and the two youngsters stared at each other. Neither felt uneasy about the other. In fact, the young rhino was very inquisitive and moved nearer.

'Be careful, son. Lion!' the mother warned him. 'I can smell it.'

The calf was about three-quarters her size and therefore much bigger than Moja. He called back, 'And I can see it, Mother Kifaru. It's tiny.'

'Not so very tiny,' Moja countered. 'At least, not for a lion.'

The adult rhino hoisted herself out of the water and lumbered towards them. Now she saw Moja properly and, seeing only a cub, imagined the rest of the pride to be nearby. 'Come on,' she said to the calf. 'Lions are bad news. We must move on and find another place to wallow.'

The calf was disappointed. He never encountered other young rhinos so the young of any creature offered some kind of compensation. 'Wait, Mother Kifaru. He's here by himself.' He turned to Moja for corroboration. 'Aren't you?'

'Yes,' Moja replied sadly. 'I lost my family a while back. I've been trying to find them.' A thought struck him. 'How did you get across the river?' he asked. 'I think I've seen you before, but not on this side.'

'We walked across, of course,' Kifaru told him. 'What a foolish question.'

Moja stared. 'Across that?' he gasped. 'But how could you?'

'It was much lower then,' the calf explained. 'Why are you so interested?' He gave a little skip which dislodged the oxpeckers.

'*I* want to cross it,' Moja explained.

'Oh. Then you'll have to wait until after the rainy season,' said Kifaru. 'Sometimes it almost dries up altogether.'

'How long will it be until then?' Moja asked at once.

'Who can tell? You'll have to be patient.'

Moja looked crestfallen. 'Is that my only chance?'

The rhino calf watched the oxpeckers flit away. 'Yes. Unless you turn into one of those.'

Moja failed to be amused. The idea of waiting for the river to dry up was just too daunting.

The young rhino tried to cheer him up. 'Don't be depressed. Can you swim?'

'Well, yes, a little, of course,' Moja replied hesitantly. 'But I've been in that water and it sort of took control of me. It was very frightening.'

'You've *been* in it?' Kifaru echoed. 'But why?'

'I had to escape from a pack of hyenas. And a leopard,' Moja added and shuddered.

'Poor young creature,' Kifaru said with sympathy. 'And no adult to help you. How long have you been on your own?'

Moja reflected and sighed deeply. 'It seems almost for ever,' he murmured sadly.

'Can't we help the little lion?' the young rhino asked his mother. He imagined what life would be like if he were on his own with no parent to protect him.

'I don't know, son,' she replied dubiously. 'What could we do?'

'Couldn't we perhaps look after him a bit? You know – until he finds his family again?'

'*You* can't look after anybody,' his mother told him. 'You have to be looked after yourself. And that's a difficult enough job with all the dangers and threats around here – drought and predators and humans with their terrifying weapons.'

'Oh, Mother. Humans with terrifying weapons? There hasn't been anything like that since I was born. You told me so yourself. The only humans I've seen have never come close. They just sit watching us.'

'It only needs one of the other kind to come back for that to change again,' Kifaru reminded him. She had lived through a period when poachers had brought rifles into the game park to slaughter rhino and elephant for horn and ivory. It was never out of her memory. 'We seem to be the last black rhinos here,' she continued, moving closer to her calf. 'I shall be content to see you grow to adulthood and independence. My job will be done then.'

Moja had listened carefully. 'Don't you have any brothers or sisters?' he asked the young rhino.

'No. No relatives,' he answered sorrowfully.

'Rhino calves are born singly,' his mother explained. 'When I was younger there were more of our kind here. But they disappeared one by one, slaughtered by men. All of them, I believe. I've never lost my fear of humans, no matter how peaceful they might seem.'

'What happened to your father?' Moja asked the young rhino.

'Slaughtered like the rest, my mother taught me. I never knew him.'

'So you're the only survivors?'

'It appears so,' Kifaru affirmed. 'And more by luck than anything else. There was a kind of battle here between different men. The ones who had done the killing were driven away before they got round to killing me and my son was born in comparative safety. Though there is never complete safety anywhere at any time. We are always vigilant.' That brought Moja's plight back to mind. 'You can stay nearby if you want to,' she told the lion cub. 'I'll do what I can for you – which isn't much. Rhinos are not provided with the best eyesight. But I can smell danger early. It might be that my bulk could deter some of your foes as well as our own.'

Moja was considerably comforted. He didn't feel quite so alone as before and he accepted the big animal's offer gratefully.

Meanwhile, on the other side of the river and some distance away, Battlescars had sighted Huru and Kimya and was hurrying towards them. The lionesses greeted him affectionately, rubbing their heads against his and sliding their bodies alongside his flanks. Battlescars reciprocated joyfully. The small pride was his favourite and now his only one. The cubs bounced around in excitement too. Eventually the inevitable question was asked by Kimya.

'Where's Blackmane?'

Battlescars flopped down on to his belly. His head dropped. 'My brother is dead,' he murmured dolefully. For a moment there was silence. The pride members were stunned. Then, in a rush, Battlescars was bombarded with questions and, while he explained about the tremendous fight with Challenger, the sisters began to notice his latest wounds.

'These are the work of that young upstart?' Huru asked with surprise. She could see that some of the wounds were the most severe Battlescars had ever suffered.

'He's no upstart now,' the old male growled in answer. 'He has learnt a thing or two and he's very strong. He killed my brother.' He turned his head and looked away towards the northern horizon. 'The large pride is no longer ours. No longer mine,' he corrected himself. 'I surrendered it without a fight. I didn't have the stomach or the heart to do battle for it without Blackmane.'

Huru was secretly delighted that they had Battlescars all to themselves now, but refrained from saying so for fear of wounding his self-esteem. But she realized that having only one adult male in the pride posed a problem. She and Kimya would have to share him. 'It's good to have you back,' was what she did say. 'We've had our work cut out looking after the cubs by ourselves.'

Battlescars looked at the youngsters properly for the first time since his return. He noticed that his biggest cub was still absent. 'Moja must be dead too,' he said resignedly.

The lionesses didn't contradict him. Kimya in fact had remained virtually silent since the first greetings were over. Blackmane had been her mate and she was truly saddened by the news of his defeat. Yet at the same time she couldn't help thinking about the powerful young male who had defeated him. Battlescars had taken punishment too so the younger lion had obviously fought heroically. She wondered what would happen if he should choose to mount a fresh challenge at some later stage. Battlescars was ageing visibly and, although victorious last time, would be seriously tested if the moment should come when he must fight on his own. Despite everything, she couldn't suppress a feeling of excitement at the prospect.

'Was the young lion badly hurt?' she asked as Huru started to lick Battlescars's gashes.

'Oh, yes. He was well and truly beaten,' Battlescars answered categorically. 'He crawled away afterwards and went into hiding. I doubt if he'll come looking for me for a while.' His confidence was returning as he spoke and he felt the loyalty of his pride members as they surrounded him.

But Kimya said, 'If he's young and strong he'll recover and he *will* come back. What else can he do? He will want a mate and a pride for himself – he will challenge again and again.'

Huru glared at her sister. 'Perhaps you'd welcome it?' she snapped, suspecting Kimya was jealous of her closer tie with Battlescars.

'No,' Kimya replied, though she wasn't really sure herself. 'I'm only speaking the truth and Battlescars knows it.'

'Yes,' he admitted. 'You are right. But I'm not done yet. I don't intend to give up my last pride. Whoever might try to take it from me will find he's got the battle of his life before him.'

7

The Sisters

For the first time there was a slight uneasiness between the sister lionesses. They continued to hunt together as always. There were hungry cubs to feed as well as themselves and Battlescars, who still demanded the best meat from their kills. The male lion was content now to move around very little. He was recuperating, and enjoying the company of the cubs who found him a more tolerant parent and play-fellow now that his interests were restricted to one pride. He showed no preference for Huru over Kimya. Neither the one nor the other was his favourite. But although the sisters had once before shared a male companion, Huru's lack of enthusiasm for him had avoided any rivalry. Now things weren't so relaxed. When Blackmane had been around Huru had had most of Battlescars's attention because Kimya had had Blackmane's. Huru believed Kimya was jealous of her now that Blackmane had gone, and she found herself watching her sister suspiciously when the pride was at rest.

The cubs were growing quickly. They were healthy and strong. Mbili and Tatu, being older, were a little bigger than Nne, Tano and Sita. All of them were inquisitive and eager to follow the hunt. Day by day they learnt more as they watched their mothers' tactics. Huru and Kimya used speed, cunning and perfect co-operation. They had become the most successful of all the hunters in the game park, and were full of confidence in themselves; not only as hunters but as parents, too, as they reared their five cubs in safety and harmony. Yet their rivalry over Battlescars had the potential to disturb the pride's equilibrium.

Many days passed before the lions stumbled across the remains of Blackmane. The entire pride had gone to the pool to drink after gorging on a kill. Shreds of hide and the unfortunate beast's skeleton were all that remained, and would have been overlooked had it not been for Battlescars's memory of the fight that had taken place there. Wisps of black mane hair were the most compelling evidence that this was all that was left of his brother. The old male was very quiet as he sniffed at the remnants. He remembered Challenger and found himself scanning the surroundings for evidence of him. But the young lion was long gone by then. Battlescars's noble head dropped between his shoulders as, with open mouth, he panted in the extreme heat. He remembered the long companionship of his brother and relived in his memory the terrible battle which had destroyed him. Now Battlescars knew he must gather his strength one more time. He sighed deeply.

'Sisters!' he called. The lionesses were drinking. 'Here's a tragic sight.'

Huru and Kimya, their jowls streaming water, strode to the spot, followed by the cubs. Kimya knew instinctively what she was looking at. 'Blackmane,' she whispered. 'How sad to see such a noble beast reduced to this.' The cubs crowded round, their boisterousness lulled for once. Sita said, 'Is that my father? Who did that to him?'

Blackmane's other cubs, Nne and Tano, were silent.

They stared at the remains, unable to identify with them. They couldn't relate the sight to the image of the powerful male lion they remembered as their father. Mbili and Tatu's ties of blood with the pitiful skeleton were less strong than their cousins'. They could only wonder at the huge skull with its massive teeth which lay underwater at the edge of the pool.

'He looks as though he's lying in wait under there,' said Tatu.

And Blackmane's open jaws, through which he had expelled his last breath, did appear to be ready to swallow something.

'Foolish cub,' Kimya muttered. To Sita she said, 'Your father was killed by another lion while fighting bravely for all of us.'

'Yes,' said Battlescars appreciatively. 'That's how it was.'

The pride walked from the waterhole. Battlescars was the last to leave. 'How I miss our comradeship,' he murmured.

Sometimes Huru and Kimya saw the cheetah Upesi, who had been a neighbour in the refuge centre, hunting in the same territory. They didn't compete for the same game. The smaller cat took less bulky prey than the lionesses and they left her alone. When prey was plentiful the cheetah lost fewer of her kills to lion. However, the ever-present hyena packs were always ready to capitalise on her hard-won successes. Upesi's cubs were growing, too. She kept them well hidden and Huru and Kimya rarely saw them. The lionesses still marvelled at Upesi's breathtaking speed in the chase. Nothing could rival her and the sisters sometimes interrupted their own activities to watch her. Battlescars, however, was unimpressed.

'Imagine using all that energy and then losing a

kill,' he grunted. 'And how often does she make one? Hunting individually is a thankless task. I should know.'

'Oh? How should you?' Huru teased him. 'I thought you only ate what we brought you.'

'That's the best arrangement,' he agreed, unperturbed. 'A lion should be left free to defend the pride, so the females must keep him well fed. But don't think I don't know about hunting. I've done my share. As young adults my brothers and I survived several seasons on our own.'

Huru and Kimya exchanged looks. They remembered *their* early days fending for themselves alone. They still had that in common. But their inseparability now was dictated by habit rather than by desire. Kimya guessed Huru suspected her of jealousy. She often felt her scrutiny when the pride was drowsing. And she *was* jealous on occasions when she imagined Battlescars was ignoring her. However, so long as the cubs' welfare was her and Huru's priority, resentment on either side remained muffled.

One day, while matters were still in this unsatisfactory state, the sisters met up with an old friend. Ratel, the honey badger who had grown up with them at Lingmere Zoo in England, had come looking for them. He, too, had been kept for a while at the Kamenza animal refuge centre before being released into the wild, and his path had crossed with the lionesses' on a few occasions since. Now he had a problem he thought they might be able to solve, and together with his mate Clicker had searched long and hard before finally locating them. At last, using the utmost caution, the badgers approached the small pride.

The cubs were lying with their mothers under an acacia tree whose umbrella shape provided a wide area of shade. The wet season was over and the day was blisteringly hot. The honey badgers had looked for Huru and Kimya mostly by night, but on this day Ratel had smelt lion and had continued the search after dawn broke. Clicker was less confident than her mate about deliberately going up to the lionesses without a reliable bolt-hole nearby.

'It'll be all right,' he kept telling her, 'they'll recognise me. They'll remember my call. You can stay back a little if you wish.'

Clicker certainly did wish, and the closer they got to the pride the further behind she dropped. Ratel began his calls: a sort of chirrup or a rattly whistle. The lions were all dozing and his cries didn't disturb them. He moved nearer.

'As soon as they see my black and white coat they'll know me,' he assured himself.

Clicker called, 'That's far enough! Be careful! There's another big lion coming to join them.' She hastily scrabbled for cover in some prickly scrub.

Ratel hadn't reckoned on the big male. Battlescars had been sleeping on his back in some grass but the heat had proved too intense and he was heading now for the shade. The lionesses woke as Battlescars padded in, giving his throaty growl of greeting. Kimya yawned and sat up. She saw the honey badger and roused Huru.

'Look, sister. Is that—'

More calls from Ratel interrupted her as the badger hurried to identify himself. Now Battlescars looked too and the cubs began to show interest.

Huru said, 'Well now, what does he want?'

'Let's go and see,' said Kimya.

'*I'll* go and see,' Battlescars snarled, already irritated by the heat. He began to run forward. Ratel looked round for cover but he was too slow. The lion bounded up and took a swipe at him. Ratel slipped to one side and squealed, 'Lions! Sisters! It's me. Quickly!'

Kimya was the first to react. She owed Ratel a favour. She had once badly wounded him by mistake, when she had mistrusted him and attacked him when he had actually been trying to help her. She ran in front of Battlescars, who was preparing to deliver another blow. 'He's a friend,' she told the male. 'An old friend from—' She was about to say 'our zoo days' but remembered that would be meaningless to Battlescars. '—from way back,' she explained. 'Before we knew you.'

Battlescars was uninterested but his aggression faded. 'Really?' was all he said in a bored tone before he strolled back to the acacia and slumped down.

'Thank you,' Ratel gasped. 'I didn't know about him.' Now he was surrounded by curious cubs who gambolled about playfully, putting out paws to pat the strange creature, then skipping off before he could react.

'Why have you come, Ratel?' Kimya asked. 'It was dangerous.'

Huru biffed the cubs away and sat down beside her sister.

'I – we – want your help,' Ratel told them. He looked behind him but failed to see Clicker, who was still hidden. 'It's all right!' he called. 'I told you.' He was aware of the irony in the remark, considering he had nearly been killed. He looked at the lionesses sheepishly. 'We've had trouble,' he continued as Clicker emerged with caution.

'What trouble?' Huru asked.

'A bird steals our food,' Ratel explained. 'A big, fierce bird with talons and a hooked beak. It can run fast overground as well as fly. It follows us and pounces on our kills. We're – we're starving. And that's not all—'

'It's a goshawk,' Clicker interrupted. She knew more about birds than Ratel. 'It sits on a branch and chants. I think it's mocking us. And we—'

'We had young,' Ratel interrupted. 'Like you, lions. We had a den in some rocks.'

'I remember it,' said Kimya.

'The bird killed the babies. It was always around. It waited and waited and got them all, one by one. We moved to another den. But it always follows us.'

'I'm sorry for you,' said Huru. 'But what can *we* do?'

'Give a show of strength, perhaps,' Ratel suggested.

'Hm. Not very effective with a bird,' Huru said. 'We have trouble ourselves with vultures.'

Kimya had been thinking. She wasn't happy in the uneasy relationship with her sister. Also she did feel she wanted somehow to make amends to Ratel for that injury in the past. Maybe this was her opportunity.

'Where is this bird?' she asked.

'Wherever we are,' Clicker answered impulsively. 'It follows us around.'

'But it's not here now, is it?' Kimya pointed out.

'No, no,' Ratel answered impatiently. 'We travelled mostly by night. What she meant was, it's always around our den.'

'And where's that?'

'A rocky place with a fig tree on top.'

Kimya's ears pricked up, and so did Huru's. It sounded very like the first den they themselves had found after their release into the game park. 'I think I know it,' said Kimya. 'Perhaps I could come to help. What do you think, sister? Could you cope with all the cubs for a while?'

Huru yawned widely, displaying her huge teeth.

Clicker scampered away again and then stopped, feeling foolish. Huru thought a spell without Kimya could be beneficial. It could serve to lessen the tension between them. But she didn't feel like making it easy for her. 'I suppose so. If you *must* go,' she said.

Ratel was delighted. 'Wonderful! Thank you, lions. Shall we leave at dusk?' he asked, turning to Kimya. 'My mate and I could take the opportunity to feed now.'

'Dusk it is,' Kimya agreed. She turned to Huru. 'It won't be for long,' she assured her. 'I'm grateful to you, sister.'

8

Great News

The honey badgers grubbed around for insects and carrion and whatever small prey they could find. Clicker made sure she was well out of reach of the pride but Ratel ignored the presence of the lions while he was busy. Only Battlescars reminded him with a half-hearted roar now and then that he didn't want the smaller animal to come too close.

Kimya was ready to move as the sun began to set. She licked her cubs fondly but she had no qualms about leaving them in Huru's care. The sisters had raised their young together, sometimes suckling each other's as well as their own. So all the cubs were just as happy with either lioness as guardian.

Ratel and Clicker trotted off in their usual sprightly way with the lioness plodding along comfortably in their wake. Every so often Clicker would glance behind to make sure she was still there and not planning some kind of trick. Kimya was perfectly content to follow and was at ease until she knew she was beyond the limits of the small pride's territory. Then she trod more quietly and kept her wits about her. The honey badgers' den was not actually very far distant; they had wasted days searching for the lionesses in the wrong direction. The three animals reached the rocky outcrop without incident and in thick darkness. Although it was a cloudy night and moon and stars were obscured, Kimya recognised fig tree rock at once.

'How strange you should have settled here,' she said. 'It holds memories for me. It was the first real den my sister and I had in this area.'

Ratel wasn't terribly interested. 'The bird will probably be perching on the fig tree as light breaks,' he informed her. 'It sits there and waits for us to stir.'

'But as you've been absent for a while perhaps it won't still be around,' Kimya suggested.

'We shall see. I doubt if it's shifted itself. It likes the way we hunt,' Ratel growled bitterly. He and Clicker scuttled into their den.

Kimya climbed up the rocks. She lay down among the old fig's trailing roots and thought for a while about Huru. She remembered how they had sheltered here together in the early days of their life in the savannah country. How close they had been then! Kimya felt sad as she pondered their present relationship. Was there an estrangement? If there was it could only be on the surface. She knew that if she were in danger Huru would be the first to come to her aid, as she would for Huru.

'Males complicate things,' she muttered, feeling the familiar twinge of jealousy as soon as Battlescars came into her mind. 'They're better off without me for the moment,' she mumbled, 'though I can't stay here for long.' Head on paws, she fell into a doze.

Day dawned bright and clear. The clouds had passed over and the temperature rose quickly. A shaft of early sunlight penetrated the sparse canopy of the stunted fig tree and fell on Kimya's face. She woke and looked up. The tree's branches were bare of bird life. 'I thought so,' she said to herself. 'The goshawk has flown.'

But she was wrong. A little later Ratel and Clicker emerged from their den. As if at a given signal the hawk zoomed in from wherever it had been roosting and found a perch in the fig from where it could watch their movements. The honey badgers pretended they hadn't noticed and set about their foraging. Kimya peered up at the bird, directly above her. The lioness was well hidden from the unsuspecting hawk, which imagined itself completely safe as it watched confidently for the appearance of food.

'That bird's going to get a nasty shock,' Ratel hissed to his mate with the greatest satisfaction. 'Our lion friend's on the top of the rock.'

Clicker said nothing. She wasn't beyond thinking that, after the lioness had dealt with the goshawk, she might turn her attention to them. She just wished for the episode to be over so that she could burrow away out of sight between the rocks where nothing could reach her.

Ratel caught a mouse and sat looking at it. He knew the bird was looking at it too. There was a flap of wings as the goshawk abruptly launched itself from its branch, followed immediately by a shriek. Kimya had reared up simultaneously and aimed a blow with one powerful paw at the swooping bird. She caught only its tail as it dived past her, but it was enough to rip out its long tail feathers. The goshawk managed to steady itself, though it corrected its flight with great difficulty, shrieking its chant-like alarm cry. However, when it sought refuge back on the topmost branch of the fig, the lack of its tail feathers upset its balance and its grip was uncertain. Screeching in panic, it tumbled from its would-be perch and crashed down through the branches, where Kimya pounced again and finished the job. Then the lioness bounded from the rock.

'You won't be troubled again,' she grunted.

Clicker showered nervous praises on her in a bid to ingratiate herself. Ratel was simply relieved. 'I knew you could do it. We're in your debt, lion.'

'No,' Kimya answered. 'It was a debt repaid. I owed you.'

Ratel knew at once what she meant. 'Well,' he said with some emotion, 'friends always now. Eh, lion?'

'Always,' said Kimya.

The goshawk's last piercing cries had attracted attention elsewhere. Other lions were calling to each other about the commotion. Kimya remembered in haste that she was a trespasser in strangers' territory.

'I must get out of here,' she told the badgers sharply. 'Can't stay a moment longer.' She sniffed the air and looked around to make sure her exit was clear. 'Goodbye, Ratel!'

Kimya sprang forward and ran. Ratel called after her, 'I hope we see each other again.' Kimya was out of earshot before he had finished but it didn't matter. She understood, and she shared his sentiments.

Clicker felt differently. 'I hope we *don't* see each other again,' she said bluntly. 'I'm not happy with lions about, despite what that one's done for us.'

'There are lions. And there are friends,' Ratel replied loftily and he began to pluck the goshawk with his powerful jaws.

Kimya crossed the alien territory in leaps and bounds. She knew the lions of the neighbourhood would be at their most alert in early morning. She was approaching familiar ground and congratulating herself on her safe passage when a male lion suddenly appeared ahead of her. She stopped short, weighing up her chances. The animal was solitary and no bigger than she was. Kimya relaxed. She had the lion's measure. Its mane told her it had barely reached full maturity. They stared at one another. The male gave a growl of greeting. Kimya didn't return it but she recognised the young lion's voice and found herself tingling with excitement. It was Challenger.

'I wondered when I'd come across you,' he said. 'I knew you'd left your pride.'

'I haven't left it,' she answered brusquely. 'Don't make that mistake.'

'Well, why are you here?'

'It wouldn't interest you to know,' she replied. 'But I can tell you that I'm returning to my family right now.'

'Of course you are,' Challenger said serenely. 'How's the male?'

'How can *you* ask such a question?' Kimya snapped. Then she groaned, remembering Blackmane with sadness.

'Well, I didn't kill both of them,' Challenger leered. 'What of the survivor?'

'He's fully recovered,' Kimya retorted. 'You needn't sound so smug. He'll be ready when you come calling again.'

'How do you know I will?' Challenger asked, amused.

Kimya realised she had almost given herself away and was annoyed. She tried to recover ground. 'Are you so easily put off?'

'Oh, no. How's your sister? Still as close as ever, the pair of you?'

Kimya blinked. The young upstart seemed to know all about her situation. Or was he guessing? 'Closer,' she fibbed. Now she saw the scars on his body and astonished herself by feeling a rush of sympathy. 'How are your wounds? Still smarting?'

'Of course they're still smarting,' he admitted honestly, 'I nearly died.'

Kimya softened. 'I'm . . . glad you didn't,' she heard herself saying. 'One death was enough.' She began to move away, aware that she had probably given the young lion encouragement without meaning to.

'Wait!' Challenger called, trying to think of something that might detain her. He came closer. 'Did your cub return?'

Kimya was puzzled. 'My cub?' Then she thought of Moja. 'You mean—' she began, then interrupted herself. 'How do you know about him?' she demanded.

Challenger started to explain. Kimya was too impatient to listen. 'You've seen him!' she exclaimed. 'Then he's alive?'

'As far as I know,' Challenger replied, and went on to describe how they had spent time together, omitting his own part in preventing Moja's return. 'I lost touch with him. I'm surprised he hasn't found you by now.'

Kimya suspected there was more to the story than she had been told. But all she could think of just then was to bring the glad news to Huru. 'Thank you for this,' she said. 'I know someone who'll be even more thrilled than I am to hear it.' And she raced on her way without a second's hesitation.

Battlescars was hungry. Huru had moved the cubs to a place of concealment while she watched a group of zebra. She needed to make a kill. The male lion shadowed her reluctantly, waiting only for Kimya's reappearance as an excuse to absent himself. Huru had no reason to trust Battlescars as a hunter – he had no flair for it – so she too looked forward to Kimya's

return. She would have been even more impatient
had she guessed at the news her sister would bring.

'Sister!' Kimya bounded up, panting and frolicking
in her high spirits. 'He's alive! Our cub's alive!'

Huru forgot all about hunting. 'Do you mean . . .
can you mean . . .' She was trembling.

'I mean Moja! Yes! He's alive and somewhere not
far away. I've been speaking to' – her voice dropped
to a whisper as Battlescars showed signs of interest –
'the brave young lion.'

Huru didn't question Kimya's motives in conversing
with Blackmane's killer. She was desperate to hear
more about Moja. 'Tell me all about it later,' she said
in a low voice as Battlescars joined them.

'Is it Moja you're talking about? Where is he? How
do you know he's still alive?' the old male demanded
eagerly.

Kimya gave him the chief facts. 'I don't know where
he is,' she finished. 'But he's feeding himself and
surviving. He must come back soon. Oh, won't the
other cubs be delighted?'

'Food first,' Battlescars decreed. 'They need to eat.
We all need to eat. Than we'll decide what to do
about Moja.'

An hour later the pride slumbered, undisturbed by
the noise of jackals and vultures competing for the
scraps remaining from the lions' repast. The cubs, as
usual, were the first to rouse and their antics quickly
awoke the lionesses. Huru and Kimya knew that now
was the time to give them the news of Moja.

'Listen, all of you!' Huru's eager voice made them
pay attention at once. 'Your brother Moja isn't lost.
He has been seen and he's healthy and coming back
to us.'

The cubs' reaction was not what she and Kimya had
expected. As time had gone on the youngsters had

stopped asking about Moja and had all but forgotten him. Now they were quiet while they tried to deal with what were only faint memories of their missing playmate. Huru and Kimya helped by reminding them of some early incidents when they had all been together. Mbili and Tatu particularly became very excited then.

'Our brother's coming! Our brother's coming!' they cried, beginning to look out for him there and then. Nne, Tano and Sita, their cousins, were drawn into the excitement.

'Wait,' said Kimya. 'He has to find us first. We don't know how far away he is. But he will come.'

'One day we'll all be together again,' Huru added.

Battlescars was aroused by the lively cubs. He began to think about Moja and how a sturdy cub who had managed to survive on his own for so long would be an asset to the defence of the pride. Battlescars had felt vulnerable since his brother's death and badly needed allies. The cubs were too young to be of any use yet, but in Moja's case there was the prospect of a male with real strength and courage that he could rely on in the future.

For Battlescars knew his days as the dominant lion were numbered. He was aware that his strength was ebbing and that soon there would be challenges to his authority that he couldn't meet. Moreover, he didn't feel like waiting on the off chance that one day Moja would find his pride. He – Battlescars – wanted to ensure it.

'It's time I went to look for Moja,' he announced suddenly. 'I shall search for him high and low until I find him.'

Huru and Kimya felt some surprise. It was unusual for an adult male to show such concern for a cub. The sisters exchanged glances, then looked at Battlescars through new eyes. He looked back at them steadily, proudly. He understood their thoughts.

'We need him here,' he said.

9

A Rescue

Moja was still longing for the day when he could cross back over the river. Whenever he could he went to look at it, willing its flow to diminish. And, with the onset of the dry season, the river's level *was* beginning to drop. But not fast enough for the fretting lion cub. Sometimes he was in such a froth of impatience that he would wonder about taking the plunge and swimming across. Then the memory of the river's power would deter him. Meanwhile he stayed close to his new friends, the black rhino calf and mother.

The rhinos preferred bush to open country on the whole. Where they went Moja followed. The two youngsters became firm companions and Moja gave the rhino calf a name: Pembe, meaning horn. The lion cub felt safe in the bush. The rhinos had no enemies now that Pembe was too big to arouse the interest of predators. So, as long as Moja didn't stray far from them, he was well protected. Small mammals, reptiles and birds were easy for him to find, but he missed the taste of richer meat: antelope, buffalo or zebra. He fretted about his family. He knew nothing about its fortunes since they had become separated. He often wondered if the pride was still together or even alive.

The cub came to hate the river although he and

the rhinos frequently drank from it. It was the one impassable barrier to fulfilling his constant dream. His vigils on its bank continued. Pembe tried to encourage him. 'The water's getting lower,' he would often say. 'Mother Kifaru says it will be fordable soon.' But when Moja went to look at it, the river always appeared the same to him. Pembe enjoyed the company of another young animal. He regretted that Moja would soon have to leave but he understood his desperation to find his family.

Battlescars was busy trying to find a trace of his son. He had one advantage: he at least knew where Moja had last been seen. Challenger had described to Kimya his meeting with Moja by the waterhole where Blackmane had died. So the old male had begun his search there. And Battlescars was not alone. There was another who was looking for Moja.

For some time at Kamenza Joel had been wrestling with his uncertainty about the cub. He thought it likely it had been killed but he hadn't verified it. Finally he felt that he ought to do so and consulted his boss Simon Obagwe.

'I can't seem to rest easy,' Joel explained. 'I'd just like to know for sure about the cub.'

'So would I,' Simon said. 'And you know how Annie feels about him. Why don't you go back to the place where you say he ran from you before? You could perhaps use more caution this time?' Simon smiled and raised his eyebrows. It was a subtle hint. 'You might pick up a clue. We know, don't we, that he isn't back with the pride?'

'Oh, yes,' Joel answered. 'I've checked that out more than once. When shall I . . .'

'You can go today,' Simon finished for him. 'There's not a great deal to do around here at present. Maybe you should take a couple of the men with you. That way you could cover more ground.'

Arrangements were made and the time fixed. Joel took two men in the Land-Rover with him, Paul and Joseph. They left the vehicle as soon as practicable, making sure it was fairly well concealed before continuing on foot. Joel headed straight for the river; the other two took more circuitous routes. Paul and Joseph were armed in case of a surprise attack by lion or other large game, but they were expert trackers and didn't expect a disturbance. Joel never carried a gun as a rule and this day was no exception. He told the other men he wouldn't stray far from the Land-Rover, and would rely on his senses. After years of working with big powerful mammals in one way or another his eyesight and hearing were acutely developed.

Joel saw nothing alarming as he trod slowly and cautiously over the ground. It was quiet. The sun glared and its heat kept most game inactive and under cover. Joel tried to ignore the discomfort but every so often he had to mop his face and neck. He slowed further as he neared the river, thinking he could detect some movement on the far bank. As he approached he saw a tawny shape which set his heart beating faster. Soon he could make out that he was looking at a well-grown lion cub. He paused and watched the young creature lie down and put its head on its paws. Joel's excitement increased. He was almost certain that this was the cub he longed to see. He needed to get just a little closer to make sure. Before doing so he glanced around to see if it was safe, and also to try to pinpoint Paul and Joseph. He couldn't see Joseph but he saw Paul on his far right and attracted his attention by waving. Paul began to move across.

A small bird, a honey guide, saw the signal too and flew towards Joel, chattering insistently. It knew of a bees' nest and wanted help to get into it to expose the fat grubs it relished. It knew help was usually forthcoming because humans liked honey. But it was to be disappointed on this occasion. Joel was irritated by the bird's fluttering around him, and particularly by its incessant chattering when he needed quiet above all things. The honey guide wouldn't be put off and Joel feared the disturbance would unsettle the young lion. Sure enough, the bird's twittering had alarmed it. The cub got up nervously. As Joel moved forward again he could see the youngster clearly and he knew straight away he was looking at Moja. The cub had been making one of his patrols on the river bank to examine the water. Joel was thrilled. He didn't waste a moment wondering how the cub had escaped the hyenas and all the other dangers he must have faced. It was enough that he had survived and appeared to be thriving. Joel felt a combination of relief and delight and he called jubilantly to Paul that their search was over.

The man's voice startled Moja. The lion cub saw two men approaching the river and a third running towards them in the distance. He fled for protection to the rhinos' side but the mother rhino was frightened by the human presence herself. Moja's alarm increased her own. She crashed out of the bush and, without thinking, charged off. Her calf Pembe, who had been feeding in a different spot, was temporarily forgotten. The young rhino, left behind, panicked completely. He thrashed about in the undergrowth, entangling himself and becoming more terrified still. Despite his own fears, Moja tried to calm him. 'Wait! You'll lose yourself in there. Follow me!' But Pembe was for the moment blind to reason. He blundered

out of the vegetation and ran pell-mell for the river
in a desperate attempt to locate his mother.

'No!' Moja cried, pursuing him. 'Not that way!'

It was all over before either animal managed to pull
back. Pembe stumbled as he descended the bank and
fell on to his side. Moja, right behind, leapt to avoid
him and once again was plunged into the river. The
current was less dangerous now but Moja's previous
experience in the water sent him wild. Giddy with
fear, his attempts to swim were awkward and purpose-
less. He was in difficulties in no time. On this
occasion, though, help was at hand. Joel and Paul
raced forward and quickly waded out to the middle
where Moja was being whirled about in an eddy. The
river had dropped to a level where the men could
keep heads and shoulders above the surface, but they
had no idea what they were going to do. Moja was no
longer small and would fight them. They knew they
might be badly clawed.

'Can you try to grab his head if I deal with his
limbs?' Joel cried.

Paul nodded and now Joseph was entering the river.
Suddenly Moja seemed to be sucked underwater. He
disappeared from sight just as Joel and Paul reached
the spot where he had been struggling. As the men
splashed and lunged for the cub, Pembe clambered
back up the bank and scooted off after his mother,
kicking up mud and grit.

Joseph reached his companions and the three grap-
pled to get hold of the heavy body. Just as Moja was
about to be swept away the men managed to get a
grip. Between them they hauled him clear and, as
Moja gulped in air, they hastened to get him ashore.
Far from fighting them, the lion cub lay slack in their
arms.

'We'd better take him back to have a look at him,' Joel said. 'He doesn't seem too good.'

'He swallowed a lot of water,' Paul remarked.

The three men strode back to the Land-Rover. Before they reached it a deep and angry roar brought them up short. Encumbered by their load they were unable to wipe their faces free of the water that streamed down them.

'Take care,' Joel warned shortly. 'That sounded too close for comfort.'

They hurried on but they were still fifty metres from the vehicle when Battlescars, roaring defiance, broke from cover and barred their path. He had been shadowing them and he wanted his son.

10

'A Brave Little Lion'

The three men and the big dark-maned lion stared at each other. Joel and his helpers knew they were in danger but they wanted to avoid using their guns. Moja lay limp in their arms, unaware of the confrontation. Battlescars made no move but it was obvious that he wasn't going to let the men get to their vehicle.

'Let's put the cub down,' Joel said. 'I think this is the father. There isn't another lion in the game park with these kinds of scars.'

They laid Moja on the ground. The cub's eyes opened, and he stirred a little and vomited a quantity of water. He seemed to recover himself, giving a kind of squeaky yelp. The call brought Battlescars forward. The lion was as wary of the men as they were of him. Joel could see that there was no chance now of getting the cub to the refuge centre. But perhaps it wasn't necessary after all. The men stepped back as the lion advanced tentatively, baring his teeth in a nervous snarl. Now Moja saw his father for the first time and he staggered to his feet, calling a muffled greeting. Battlescars sniffed at him and looked back at the men. He decided they weren't presenting a threat.

Joel, Paul and Joseph had ample time to admire the still magnificent male and to witness a very unusual scene. Father and son, after completing the rituals of recognition, began to show real affection to each other. Battlescars nuzzled the cub. Moja butted the big male, brushing his head and body against him repeatedly. All the while a low throaty growl, evidently one of pleasure, could be heard coming from Battlescars. Joel was satisfied. Better for Moja to be with his own kind now that it seemed he hadn't suffered lasting harm.

Paul and Joseph grinned broadly at one another. Joel said, 'This is wonderful. It's a reunion. That cub has been missing for a long time.'

'I wonder, will they go together?' Paul murmured.

They were soon to find out. Battlescars had all but forgotten the men and Moja had shown no awareness of them since his recovery. The old male was ready to move. He turned and began to walk away. Moja followed instinctively. He was a little wobbly at first but soon found his strength again. Battlescars passed the Land-Rover with a cursory glance and walked on. Moja trotted behind. The men were free to reclaim their vehicle. Joel hesitated a few moments longer. He was enjoying the experience.

'He's taking the cub back to his pride,' he whispered joyfully. He looked at his companions. 'Come on. Let's get going,' he said. 'What a story we have to tell.'

Once well away from the humans the lion and his cub could relax. Moja hadn't quite come to terms with his father's abrupt appearance on the scene. He asked about it.

'I came looking for you,' Battlescars told the surprised cub. 'You're a brave little lion. I shall need you soon. I've no support any more.'

Moja was thrilled by his all-powerful father's

compliments. He still thought of Battlescars as invincible and so to be looked upon as a future ally was the highest kind of praise. 'I've tried so long to get back,' he said. 'Are my brothers and sisters all right?'

'All well. And your mother too,' Battlescars replied. 'We've had no losses apart from my brother. We've lived well. But you've had adventures, haven't you? You must tell us all about them.'

They were comfortable walking together. Moja almost felt that his father was treating him as an equal. He was proud of his new stature. Battlescars, meanwhile, was confident that the pride wouldn't have moved far without him. He found it easily and Moja, his heart almost bursting with joy and excitement, ran to meet his relatives.

Huru could scarcely credit what she saw. She knew Moja at once although he had grown handsomely since his disappearance. She licked and nuzzled him as he collapsed against her with a blissful sigh. Kimya and the other cubs greeted him with delight while Battlescars sat back and watched. It was noticeable that, because of his experiences on his own, Moja looked harder and more muscular than his siblings.

'Tell us what happened.'

'Where have you been?'

'Did you have to fight?'

The other cubs, breathless for news, demanded to know all about Moja's exploits. He was only too happy to tell them and understandably permitted himself to embellish some of his adventures.

'You've been lucky,' Huru told him afterwards. 'You've survived and there's no doubt you deserve credit for that. You've had to learn the hard way. But now we're reunited we need to stay together for our own good. I don't want you to stray any more.'

'That's all I ask: to be with you all,' Moja said.

'You'll never know how much I longed for family and companionship.' A brief flash of memory brought Pembe and Kifaru into his mind but was soon obscured by the more important concerns of his pride.

'We have to hunt today,' Kimya said to him. 'From what you tell us about eating reptiles and mongoose and scraps like that I guess you'll welcome some real meat.'

Moja drooled at the prospect. He looked forward to the time when he could actually take part in the hunt rather than just following it. But he knew that day was quite a way off yet.

'We can catch you some spiders and moths,' his sister Tatu teased him. 'You're used to things like that.'

'Flies and bugs are better,' said Mbili. 'There's more of them.'

'What about scorpions?' chimed in Nne. 'They'd be more to Moja's taste, wouldn't they?'

'Worms,' said Sita.

'Beetles,' cried Tano. 'Those big round ones that walk backwards pushing dung-balls.'

'All right; that's enough,' Moja growled. But he was amused despite himself. 'I'm a meat eater just like you, you know.' He pounced on his cousins and boxed them playfully. He was so happy to be back amongst them.

Joel, Paul and Joseph arrived back at the refuge centre. Joel sprinted up the steps to the veranda of the Obagwes' house. Simon and his wife Emelda were sipping cool drinks in the shade, waiting for the car bringing Annie back from school.

'You look as though you're about to burst,' Simon said to Joel with a chuckle. 'Good news?'

'Yes. Very,' Joel panted. 'The missing cub is alive and well and he's back with his pride. Oh, I wish Annie was here!'

'She soon will be,' Emelda said. 'Where did you see the cub?'

Joel told them everything. Simon was fascinated by the encounter with Battlescars. 'That's an amazing thing,' he commented. 'It was probably only a set of coincidences but it really sounds as if he came to fetch his youngster and then claimed him from you. I would love to have seen that.'

When Annie returned, her parents allowed Joel the privilege of retelling his story. The little girl was ecstatic and skipped about, crying, 'I knew he was alive; I knew it!' Then she flung herself on her father. 'Daddy, *please* won't you take me to see him now? I'll be so glad to see him with his mother again.'

'Of course we'll go,' said Simon. 'Joel will tell us the best time. He'll keep an eye on the pride for us.' He looked at his deputy, who nodded. 'Your mother ought to come too,' Simon continued. 'We'll make it a family trip to see a family: a lion family.'

Annie was thrilled but impatient. 'When, Joel? When?' She grasped his arm in her hands as though to drag him out there and then.

'Perhaps when it's a little cooler,' he told her with an affectionate smile, 'so long as the pride doesn't move too far off. And I must know it's quite safe for you when we go. You do understand that, don't you, Annie?'

'Oh, yes,' she crowed. She was so excited. 'Thank you. Oh, thank you.'

It didn't get any cooler. The dry season was in full swing and temperatures were high and getting higher by the day. A low wind blew which gave no relief. It seemed to scorch the air and the land like a breath from a furnace. It wasn't the sort of breeze that was usually experienced at this season. Men and animals began to wonder what it meant. The earth dried to an abnormal hardness. Trees and bushes began to drop some of their leaves as they went into a state of suspended animation. The lions of the small pride, like the rest of the inhabitants of the game park, bore with the extreme weather. They slept through most of it in whatever shade they could find, grumbling and squabbling amongst themselves for the best shelter.

The conditions didn't improve the edgy relationship that had formed between Huru and Kimya. Battlescars always demanded the shadiest spot and got it. Huru tried to get alongside him but sometimes her sister got there first. Then there was resentment or sullenness that the stifling weather fanned into really bad temper. Sometimes the cubs bore the brunt of the latter, except for Moja who, since his spell of solitude, seemed set apart. There was a kind of distance about him, almost a mystique. Battlescars always looked to see where he was before he slept. The preference he showed Moja helped to mark the young lion out.

Hunting was particularly exhausting at this time. The lionesses continued to co-operate where the essential business of food was concerned. They worked together by instinct, almost without thinking about it. After making a kill they were often so tired that they collapsed by the side of the carcass while Battlescars and the cubs ate their fill.

Once again the problem of finding water became acute. This was the sisters' second dry season in the wild, however, and they had the benefit of experience. To begin with they were able to visit a selection of waterholes. As always the smaller pools dried quickly. They relied then on the larger ones, including the one where Huru and Kimya had first joined Battle-scars and formed the small pride. Many kinds of animals used this pool: baboons often congregated there when no lions were about, while gazelle, buffalo, zebra and wildebeest regularly drank there. Upesi the cheetah and her cubs were sometimes seen. Elephant and rhino mother and calf drank the water and bathed or wallowed. Moja took care never to go near the elephant gathering. He had not forgotten how near he had come to being killed. Indeed every other animal gave way before the huge beasts when they were intent on bathing.

Moja was thrilled when his friend Pembe turned up with his mother. He ran to greet them. 'So you found each other again,' he cried in delight.

'No thanks to the men,' Pembe grunted. 'And you . . . you saved yourself?'

'No. I would have drowned. Men pulled me out, I think. But my father rescued me from them. Did you walk across the river again?'

'Yes, of course,' Kifaru answered. 'It's no problem now. You could do it.'

'But I don't want to,' Moja said. 'I'm back with my family and I'm so happy. I told my mother how you helped me.'

The big rhino turned and bent her huge head down to the cub's level so that her horns almost brushed his face. But her little eyes were soft. 'I'm so glad,' she said tenderly. 'Where is your mother?'

'She is coming this way,' Moja told her as he noticed Huru and Kimya moving slowly towards them.

Kifaru's head reared and she turned quickly to face the lionesses. At first she was unsettled. Then she recognised them. 'Ah, yes. I remember,' she murmured. 'We helped each other before.' Despite her feeling of reassurance, though, she still kept her bulk in front of her son as a screen.

After a moment the memory came to Huru too. When her cubs were only a few weeks old Challenger and his brothers had made their first attempt to steal the sisters from their mates, and the black rhino had intervened to drive them away. Her action had been in defence of her own young calf, but a bond had been forged between the three mothers.

'You were good to my son,' Huru said now. 'Thank you. He may not have survived without your friendship.'

'And we would do the same for yours,' Kimya told the rhino. 'We have an understanding.'

'I know,' she replied. 'My calf and your cub are friends. It's good to see friendship between different animals. It is men who are our enemies.'

Huru and Kimya had another view on that because of their early life. But they guessed Battlescars would be in agreement. The old male was watching the group with curiosity. He wasn't party to this association and he held himself ready to give aid to Moja should he be threatened. After a while the sister lionesses moved away and Kifaru lowered herself into some cooling mud. Moja and Pembe were left on their own. Battlescars continued to watch guardedly. Pembe dwarfed the lion cub and the big male was suspicious.

'Shall we bathe?' Pembe asked his friend.

Moja had no such inclination. 'I hate wetting my fur,' he answered. 'Besides, water has hardly been kind to me.'

'In this heat all I can think of is getting into water,' Pembe told him. 'How else can you get relief?'

'I don't know,' Moja replied. 'Perhaps the heat won't last.'

'Don't fool yourself,' Pembe said. He was older by several seasons than the lion cub. 'It could get worse yet.'

Moja felt the sun burning his back and couldn't imagine how anything could be worse. But Pembe would be proved right and, as well as the heat, another menace would arrive to test the animals even further.

──11──

Flies

The exceptionally hot dry weather had provided perfect conditions for insects. Large numbers of biting flies moved around the game park attacking any and every warm-blooded creature that could be reached. Some areas were worse than others, but in the daylight hours there were very few animals who could expect any kind of respite from their assaults. Only those with thick leathery hides like elephants, rhinos or hippos were relatively unscathed, and even these had their eyes, ears and nostrils attacked by the vicious insects. Hippos stayed submerged in the bigger pools for as long as they could; water offered the only real refuge from the tormentors. However, all the pools were now drying at an alarming rate, whilst the horrible scorching wind seemed to blow new swarms of biting insects into the park with each gust. Every beast and many a bird, too, was susceptible and made miserable in the extreme. It was difficult to eat, to hunt, to rest. The big herds started to leave the plains for fresher pasture, but on their long trail they were attacked and bitten mercilessly at every step. Weak or injured animals fell by the wayside. These were greedily snapped up by predators who themselves were weakened by the flies' attacks and lacked the energy to chase their prey.

The small pride relied on such casualties as much as any. Amongst their number Battlescars was the worst affected by the insect hordes, because some of his wounds had still not entirely healed. Any scratch, any cut, any gash, any opening in the skin at all was a magnet to the flies. Battlescars suffered terribly. Sometimes he stood up to his neck in water for hours at a time just to give himself temporary relief. Old enmities were forgotten, overtaken by more extreme considerations. More than once Battlescars and Challenger found themselves drawn to the same waterhole by the need for respite. Challenger's wounds had met with the same cruel attention as his foe's. The lions eyed one another as their sores eased just a little in the coolness of the water. Neither of them could help feeling a twinge of sympathy for the other.

'It's just merciless, isn't it?' Battlescars commented on one occasion.

'Merciless and endless,' Challenger answered. 'What we need is a plague of birds to get rid of the plague of flies.'

Even while they were speaking clusters of black biting flies buzzed round their heads. 'It would help,' Battlescars agreed. He snapped repeatedly at the black cloud that tried constantly to settle on him. 'Birds alone wouldn't be enough, though. I think it'll need something more powerful than that to do the trick.'

When the small pride was trying to rest, Huru and Kimya tried to protect the cubs by making them lie at a distance from Battlescars, because he attracted the insects so much more. But Moja liked to lie near his father and he was loath to change this habit.

'Keep away from your brothers and sisters, then,' Huru told him. 'Don't bring them any more discomfort.'

Battlescars said, 'It's better you keep away. I don't want you to suffer like me.'

The old male was losing heart. He was growing thin as they all were but in his case the continual bombardment of bites was making him dull and listless. Only at night was there any hope of peace. Each day Battlescars longed for darkness to arrive and he began to look for places to hide in during the daytime. As he endured the daily torment he witnessed the sufferings of other animals and their attempts to find relief. Amongst these he saw the cheetah family using their supreme speed to escape from their tiny attackers.

'If only I could run like that,' he muttered to himself. 'I wonder if it has any effect?' Then he thought of another aspect. 'Imagine having to use such energy in this terrible heat.'

Huru and Kimya had seen the cheetahs' tactics too. They had come across Upesi carrying part of the carcass of a young impala that had collapsed and died. The sisters had been after the same meat but Upesi had arrived on the scene first. Swarms of flies had settled on the carcass and now a cloud of them were all around the cheetah mother. As usual Upesi suspected the lionesses of wanting her find. Huru and Kimya made no move to grab it. While the flies were concentrating on Upesi the sisters were worried less. Upesi walked on tenterhooks, glancing at the lionesses and expecting them to rush at her. When they didn't she gave a muffled call to her cubs who appeared as if from nowhere out of their hiding-places. Suddenly Upesi sprang forward and began to run. The cubs followed her at once. All three cheetahs stretched their long limbs into the kind of pace that left every other kind of animal way behind.

'They're trying to shake off the flies,' Kimya breathed, in awe once again of the spotted cats' speed.

The sisters watched where they ran and saw where they dropped to the ground when they were unable to sustain their pace any longer.

'I suppose they can eat in comfort now,' Kimya said.

'I'm not so sure,' Huru mused. 'Let's go and see. We might learn something.'

'Oh, what's the point?' Kimya growled. 'We can't run like cheetahs.'

'Perhaps we don't need to. I'm going anyway,' Huru told her.

Upesi and her cubs were still trying to regain their breath. The meat was untouched when Huru arrived. Upesi snatched it up again. There were certainly fewer flies. But as Huru watched, the insects gathered again, drawn by the smell of the carcass and the cheetahs' overheated bodies.

'Is it worth it?' Huru grunted as Upesi's cubs got to their feet and took refuge behind their mother.

Upesi understood and let the meat fall. 'Some moments' respite,' she explained. 'No,' she added sullenly. 'It isn't worth it and we can't keep it up. Whatever can we do?'

'If I knew I wouldn't have come looking now,' Huru answered.

'It's torture,' Upesi moaned. 'For all of us.'

'Yes,' replied Huru grimly. 'For all of us.'

Yet there were a few animals who actually managed to avoid the misery of the flies almost altogether, the ones who lived underground and were mostly nocturnal, such as the honey badgers. Huru and Kimya watched Battlescars's increasingly desperate efforts to find a darkened spot to hide himself away during the daytime and were full of compassion, although their first concern had to be for their cubs. Eventually an idea occurred to Kimya. She had had her first litter in a rocky place where there were underground chambers ideal for a mother with new-born young. The area had also been used by Ratel and there had been trouble because of it, but now Kimya and Ratel were friends again. The honey badgers' new den at fig tree rock would be even better as a shelter for the cubs if there was sufficient room – and if the badgers were willing – because she knew there were no other occupants. 'A favour in return for a favour,' she murmured. 'So it goes on.' She mentioned the idea to her sister.

'Worth a try,' said Huru. 'It could work well. But room for all the cubs? I don't know.'

'Let's investigate then,' said Kimya. 'Should we tell Battlescars?'

Huru reflected. 'Perhaps not. He might try to take precedence as the adult male. Especially as he's in such torment.'

'That's what I think,' Kimya said. 'It seems unkind but we have to do our best for the cubs.'

The sisters waited until dusk, the time which Battle-scars used to catch up on sleep. They told the cubs where they were going and the poor youngsters were thrilled to learn there might at last be an end to their misery. Kimya led off, followed by the cubs, with Huru bringing up the rear. Moja cast several glances behind. Eventually he said, 'Isn't my father coming?'

'No,' Huru replied. 'It's better he doesn't.'

'But why?' Moja wanted to know. 'He's suffering more than any of us. Why can't he—'

'We don't think there will be room for any adults,' Kimya told him firmly.

'We can't just leave him there. How will he know where we are?' Moja persisted.

'Now look,' said Kimya sharply, 'never mind about your father. He'll survive. Your mother and I are concerned for you cubs. We have to get you some shelter.'

Huru said, 'Once you're all settled one of us will return to tell him what we've done.'

Moja wasn't happy and started to lag behind. Huru scolded him once or twice, baring her teeth, but he wouldn't hurry up and in the end she left him to his own devices. Moja's adventures had loosened the ties of parental discipline and Huru accepted it. The lionesses shepherded the other cubs between them and the youngsters trotted along dutifully while Moja slipped even further behind. Finally loyalty made him double back to arouse his father.

At first Battlescars was irritable at having his slumbers interrupted. But he soon changed his tune when he heard what Moja had to tell him. 'You were right to come back, son,' he said. 'Those females! Don't they care a jot for my welfare? Look at my hide. Look at my face.'

Moja knew only too well what ravages the flies had wreaked on his father's body where his wounds hadn't healed. Sores had become infected on his cheeks and flanks. Some still bled. His shaggy face was swollen with bites. 'Poor Father,' Moja said quietly. His own discomfort was as nothing by comparison. 'Perhaps there will be some cover for you too. We'd better hurry to catch the others up because I don't know the way.'

Kimya had pressed on ahead because she had caught the sound of the honey badgers' whistling calls. She knew they were most active at this time and guessed they were out looking for food. When she reached the den there was no sign of them. She sniffed at various entrances in the rocks and at one of them picked up Ratel's familiar smell. Kimya called softly so as not to cause alarm. There was no answer. She sat on her haunches and yawned. Maybe this was all to the good. In the badgers' absence the lion cubs could explore the rock holes and establish themselves in the best place before there was any argument.

'Ratel won't be able to complain,' Kimya told herself smugly, 'and I can soon mollify him if necessary with my sister's help.'

Huru came up with the cubs. They began to frolic about, chasing one another up and down the rocks. Mbili and Nne climbed to the lone fig tree on the top. 'Are you sure this is all right?' Huru said. 'We're outside our own territory.'

'I know. But the cubs will be out of sight in the daytime.'

Huru looked doubtful. 'When you were last here were there signs of other lions?'

'Er – yes. Well, I heard some,' Kimya admitted.

'It's a long way back if there's trouble,' Huru said.

'These aren't normal times, sister,' Kimya said. 'Look at Battlescars. He seems as weak as a new-born cub. If he's anything to go by, any other lions around here will hardly be bothering with us.'

'He isn't anything to go by,' Huru answered. 'He's much worse off than most. But I see what you mean.'

'Shall we carry on then? See what kind of cover there is here?'

Huru called the cubs together and looked at Kimya. 'Lead on, sister.'

Kimya went to the widest opening and put her head in. She eased her body through while the cubs clustered around excitedly. 'Shelter for you all here,' she announced to the youngsters, 'and maybe for one of us as well.'

The cubs scrambled to be the first through the

entrance. 'You'd better go in and quieten them down,' Kimya said to her sister. 'I can see the badgers returning.'

At first Ratel was so pleased to see the lioness that he hastened to greet her. Clicker as usual kept her distance and watched Kimya warily. Ratel whistled. 'Well, lion, this is a welcome surprise.'

'There's a reason for it,' Kimya said. 'My sister and I have brought our cubs here to escape the flies. I would have asked you first but you weren't here.'

Ratel glanced about. 'Escape the flies? Cubs? What cubs?' he chattered.

'They're hiding. With my sister. In a hole in the rock.'

'What? Oh, no! Not in our den. Oh no, lion, this isn't fair.' Ratel was very upset.

'I don't think it *is* your den,' Kimya assured him. 'Don't you use *this* one? I can smell your scent.'

'Yes, yes, that's ours. But where are you . . . oh, there. But you see, lion, my mate won't be happy about this. She doesn't trust big cats. She's very timid. Look at her. She won't even come close now. Oh, dear. No, I don't think this will work.' He lowered his voice. 'I don't want to lose her, you know, lion.'

Just then Clicker gave a series of alarm calls and scuttled for the safety of her den as she saw Moja and the looming shape of the big old male behind him. Ratel saw them too. 'More of you? Oh, I can't believe it. I know I asked you a favour and you did us a great service, lion. I'm the first to admit it. But this is too much to ask. Really. We've had to move dens more than once already.'

'Can't you stop that racket?' Battlescars bellowed at the badger irritably as he came up to them. 'Chatter, chatter.' He turned to Kimya. 'Where are the cubs? They'll have to shove up a bit if I'm to join them.'

'You can't join them,' Kimya snapped. 'There's no room.'

'We'll see about that,' Battlescars growled. He put his nose through the entrance where he could plainly hear cub sounds, but it was soon apparent to him that there *wasn't* room and he withdrew his head sharply. 'There must be other refuges here,' he muttered. 'I simply can't take any more punishment from those insects. I need a shelter and I'm going to have one.' He nosed about at other holes. Ratel was beside himself.

'No! Don't go to that one,' he cried. 'That's our den. Clicker! Are you all right?' He turned to Kimya beseechingly. 'Please, lion, can't you make him understand?'

Luckily for Clicker their den was too small for Battlescars and he plodded back and forth, searching everywhere. 'There's only one suitable,' he announced with finality at length. 'Someone's going to have to give way.' He stood by the entrance to the cubs' hole, bristling with bad temper. Huru emerged without a word and stood, sniffing the air inquisitively.

Ratel had caught the same scent. 'Maybe you'll all have to give way,' he said, not without satisfaction. 'You're out of your own patch and I can smell the lions of the woodland pride.'

——12——

Tyranny

Kimya bounded up to the top of the rock. It was too
dark to see far into the distance, but there were defi-
nite signs of movement on the plain below. Greyish
shapes of perhaps three or four animals were
approaching steadily. She knew they were lions. The
way they moved was unmistakable, even before one
of them called. Kimya scurried down to rejoin her
sister. The lionesses were in a quandary. They couldn't
decide whether to back themselves against the rock
refuge, so protecting the cubs, or to gather the youngsters for flight.

'What shall we do, sister?' Kimya demanded tensely.
'The lions are close.'

'I . . . I . . .' Huru stammered.

'Run!' Battlescars cried peremptorily. He was
assuming authority instinctively. That was his role.
'Take the cubs and run to our territory. It was a
mistake, bringing them here. I see it now. Get going!
I'll deal with things here. I used to hold this woodland
pride. I know them all as well as I know you. The
males are novices!'

The sisters knew better. Battlescars and Blackmane
had been ousted by these very youngsters shortly after
the end of the last dry season, but there was no time
to argue. Huru called the cubs sharply. 'Mbili, Tatu,

we're leaving! Nne, Tano, Sita, come quickly. Now!'
Almost without thinking, his mother omitted Moja's
name. She knew he would remain with his father.

The cubs came tumbling from the hole in the rocks,
looking scared. Ratel added his own prompting. 'Run
swiftly, youngsters, and don't come back here. It's not
safe.'

Battlescars took up his stance, facing the enemy,
and drawing himself up to his full height. For all his
setbacks, he was still an imposing-looking beast. Huru
and Kimya, the cubs between them, fled without a
backward glance. Only Moja stood with his father, but
Battlescars ordered him to take cover. 'You're not
ready for this, my son. Hide yourself and watch. You
may learn a thing or two.'

Moja was filled with pride by his father's bravery.
Despite Battlescars's recent sufferings, his innate
courage hadn't left him. The cub backed into the big
rock entrance as Ratel scuttled to his den to join
Clicker.

The woodland lions came on the scene: two males
and two females, the most senior of the pride lionesses. Battlescars quickly noticed that they were all in
very poor condition, worse even than himself. He
gained confidence immediately. One of the males he
recognised as having taken a lesser role in driving
himself and his brother out of the pride all those
months ago. It was exceptionally skinny-looking. The
other male walked with a limp. A wound on one of
its feet hadn't healed and the paw was very badly
swollen. The females looked downcast and hopeless.
The four looked at Battlescars as he looked at them.

'You've come to remind me I'm out of bounds,'
Battlescars said ironically. 'But I doubt if you can
enforce your boundaries.'

'Boundaries are meaningless now,' said the skinny

male. 'We picked up your scent and decided to consult you. We're at the end of our tether. Our woodland is teeming with flies. We can't survive there. Look at us.'

'I have looked. Where's the rest of the pride?'

'Around,' replied one of the females. 'Too weak to move any more.'

Battlescars's sympathy was profound. He knew all these beasts; he had mated with this very lioness. He remembered also when these two males were mere youngsters. 'As you can see, I've suffered dreadfully too. No lion has escaped the misery. I thought I was the most wretched of all animals. Now I see that I'm not.'

'What can be done?' the limping lion begged. 'We shall die.'

'There will be deaths soon,' Battlescars agreed. 'I don't know the answer any more than you. I'm here because I'm desperate for shelter. Amongst these rocks there is some kind of refuge.'

The males hung their heads. Fighting for any refuge was out of the question. They were without hope. They lay down with the females in a huddle. Even walking this far had drained their strength completely.

'I really wish I could help you,' Battlescars said with genuine concern. 'There's a terrible blight on us all.' He turned sorrowfully and nudged Moja further into the hole, following him in. 'The males look utterly beaten,' he told the cub. 'Insects have accomplished what I and my brother were unable to do.'

When daylight slanted into the gloom of their refuge, Moja left his father sleeping and peered out. The woodland lions were no longer there. Ratel was crunching up a beetle outside his den. 'They shuffled off,' he told the cub. 'Very sorry for themselves, they seemed. Why don't you and the big lion go too? Leave Clicker and me in peace.'

'I'll stay as long as *he* wants to,' Moja answered stubbornly. He heard Battlescars stirring and went back inside to tell him they were alone.

'Good,' said Battlescars. 'I didn't feel comfortable with those poor brutes around. Now it's different and I'll stay right here.'

'You mean—'

'I mean just that. Right here in this hole.'

'But there's no food here,' Moja said. 'How will you eat?'

'Something's likely to come by now and then,' Battlescars replied confidently. 'I'll be ready. This is where I'll be until those flies leave off pestering me.'

Moja was worried. He thought his father's wits had deserted him. He resolved there and then to look after him as far as he was able, even if the flies never gave up.

It seemed they never would. Although the hot dry wind had blown itself out, the clouds of biting flies were ever present. Because of their thick hides Pembe the rhino calf and his mother Kifaru had been troubled less than most animals to begin with. Browsing was the main problem for them. As they cropped leaves and twigs the flies got into their mouth parts. This was horrible, but it didn't deter them from eating. Then one day, feeding from a thorn tree, Kifaru caught her long upper lip on a really sharp spike and tore it. The wound was an immediate target for the tormentors. No matter how much she swung her head the flies held fast and more and more collected around her mouth. The rhino didn't have the temperament or the fortitude of a big cat. She was nervous and jumpy and the insects' bites maddened her. She plunged about the bush, rocking and bucking her great body to no effect. Pembe tried to keep up with her.

'Mother, the waterside. Let's go to the wallow!' he cried.

Cooling mud was the only remedy. In normal circumstances she would have thought of it herself but now she was crazed. She charged away, running full tilt for the nearest waterhole. Pembe followed. Unfortunately, the pool had almost completely dried up; there was no wet mud to offer relief. Almost without stopping to register the fact, the rhinos careered onwards to a larger pool. There was water here but only cracked and crusted earth on its margins. Kifaru crashed on to her side and rolled on the ground in a vain attempt to find mud, but all was hard and stony. Heaving to her feet, she dashed into the water, scattering the other creatures that were trying to use it as a sanctuary. The pool's depth was severely depleted and the water only reached to Kifaru's knees. She lowered her head beneath the surface and at last the flies shifted. Kifaru and Pembe drank gratefully. But as soon as Kifaru's head was free of the water again, the insects were back. They had been circling and waiting. There was one last hope: the river.

Snorting furiously, Kifaru wheeled round and broke into a gallop. She headed straight for the river. But she never got there. With her head bent and her eyes almost closed to keep out the maddening insects, she thundered across the ground, veering neither to right nor left. A huge baobab tree stood in her path and with an agonising *crump* she blundered right into it with all the force of her tonnage moving at top speed. The mighty tree shuddered at the impact. Kifaru's head was crushed and the poor tormented

creature toppled over like a dislodged boulder and
lay perfectly still. Pembe stared at the body. He butted
and nudged it. He couldn't understand at first what
had happened. But when he saw his mother's battered
face and shoulders he did begin to comprehend and
he gave squeals of distress. Pembe was over three years
old and would soon have been completely indepen-
dent of his mother, yet in his brief life he had never
known anything other than her constant companionship and nurture. He was bereft.

For a long time he stayed near Kifaru's body. He
had never felt so dreadfully alone. As far as he knew
no other rhinos inhabited this savannah country. He
had no relatives and no friends. Then he remembered
Moja. The lion cub had been a friend of sorts and
Pembe had enjoyed having him around. But where
was he now? Pembe hadn't seen him for a while. The
cub was back with his own kind and that was how it
should be. Before that, however, Moja had been on
his own for a long time. Pembe was struck by the
similarity of the situation that had so suddenly been
thrust upon him. Moja knew what loneliness felt like.
How comforting it would be to be with him now.

Pembe lay down by Kifaru's side. His grief was too
strong at that moment to allow him to do anything
but mourn her. But it was in his mind to find Moja
when he should feel able to leave his mother.

Simon Obagwe the game warden, his family and his
staff knew all about the fly infestation. Not only the
heat but the insects too had prevented Annie from
taking her trip to see Moja and the pride. Humans
weren't immune from the nuisance, but at least they
had the means to repel the worst attacks. It was difficult to do much about the suffering of the animals.
Vegetation could be sprayed from the air but it was

an expensive operation. In any case, the whole of the game park seemed to be affected and that was too large an area to deal with properly. It would take weeks. Moreover, the animals themselves, of course, couldn't be sprayed. Simon was hard pressed to know what to do for the best.

He and his staff made frequent journeys into the game park, each time to a different area, in an effort to keep tabs on the problem and to see whether there were any signs of its diminishing. On one of these trips they found the dead rhino. Simon was very concerned for Pembe, who by that time had moved on. It was particularly important that he should thrive because a young female rhinoceros was being cared for in the refuge centre as she was prepared for eventual release into the wild. She had been transported from another game park specifically as a potential mate for Pembe. Over time Simon wanted to build up a viable breeding stock of black rhino in his area, but the programme would have to be shelved until the insect scourge had been overcome.

Pembe knew nothing of all this. He was trying to manage on his own. He was not at risk from predators; he was approaching full size and there were currently no hunters with the strength needed to tackle a rhinoceros. But he wasn't used to solitude and each day he hoped to catch a glimpse of Moja. His wanderings after the best browse, a pattern taught him by his mother, eventually took Pembe to a bush area not far from fig tree rock. Then it was Moja who spotted him, rather than the other way round.

Moja had been true to his word. He had remained with his father for several days. During that time they had eaten a spring hare and a small snake between them. Moja tried constantly to get Battlescars to move from his shelter but his father refused to budge.

'You mustn't stay with me,' he told Moja. 'There's no need. Go back to the pride. Tell them I'll come when my wounds have healed properly.'

'You'll starve,' Moja warned him. 'I can't hunt proper game and you won't. How long can you last?'

Battlescars only emerged to drink from the marshy area nearby and always at night. He expected to find prey there, but there never seemed to be any. The honey badgers were becoming increasingly nervous. They begged Moja to persuade Battlescars to go.

'I'm trying, I'm trying,' he told them. 'He's deaf to all appeals. I think hunger will drive him out in the long run.'

'Unless he eats us first,' Clicker wailed. 'We can't rest, hearing those horrible rumblings from his great belly day after day.'

Moja hid his amusement, though he understood their worries. He decided at least to try to catch a worthwhile meal and it was when he was heading for a wooded area that he spotted Pembe. He was astonished to see the young rhino on his own and ran up to him at once. Pembe was overjoyed to see him.

'This is so good, you being here,' the rhino said with delight. 'I've wanted to see you for ages.'

'But where's your mother? Where's Kifaru?' Moja asked.

'Gone,' Pembe murmured, and he told the cub all about the tragedy.

Moja was shocked. He could scarcely grasp what he was hearing. That such a big, powerful animal could be driven to her death by insects was almost incredible. 'What an awful story,' he muttered. Then, unnecessarily, 'So you're on your own?'

'Not any more,' Pembe answered brightly. 'Oh, I'm so glad to have a friend to talk to.'

Moja felt a little awkward. Pembe was his friend and he was pleased to see him, but his own place was with lions. He couldn't provide the rhino with company permanently. He had already made a commitment to his father and now another animal wanted to rely on him as well. At that moment Moja wished fervently he was back with his pride, just one cub among many.

As though he had read Moja's thoughts, Pembe said, 'Why are *you* alone, anyway?'

Moja explained. Then Pembe said, 'It's all right. You don't have to stay with me all the time. We're all facing the same tiny enemy. It's like a kind of tyranny. I suppose flies have enemies too that will come some time to release us.'

They were prophetic words. There was an enemy waiting in the wings, but it would prove to be an enemy not only to the flies.

13

'The Start of Something'

Extreme heat, dust, flies. The animals were at the end of their tether. The migratory herds had departed, leaving the residents of the plains to bear the brunt of the gruelling conditions. By now Huru and Kimya were enjoying their old relationship again: sisters united by struggle and suffering. With Battlescars absent, so was rivalry. Somehow they kept the cubs fed, and they continued to groom them as best they could. Huru hardly had time to spare a thought for Moja.

Early one morning the lionesses woke and smelt a strange scent. They got to their feet, sniffing the air as they did so.

'What is it?' Kimya asked. The smell was sharp and sour.

Huru was puzzled too, yet she was reminded of something in her past. The memory was faint. Gradually the smell became more reminiscent. It was similar to one she had occasionally traced at the zoo in England when the wind had carried cooking smells to the lionesses' enclosure from the small restaurant there. She didn't know what it meant now.

'Nothing we need to bother about,' she said.

The cubs were curious as well. Although they weren't aware of it, the smell made them salivate. The lionesses noticed.

'It's meat,' said Kimya. 'That's what it is.'

'What kind of meat?' Huru queried. It didn't resemble anything they had been used to.

'Good meat,' said Mbili. 'It smells good.'

The cubs' hunger was a constant worry to the sisters in their weakened state. Huru thought the smell was worth investigating. Perhaps there was carrion to be had if the hateful hyenas hadn't beaten them to it. Anyway, they couldn't afford to pass up this kind of chance. She looked at her sister. Kimya was drooling. Huru realised that her own mouth was running with water. Without another word she led the cubs away, Kimya in the rear this time.

It was a simple matter to follow their noses. The cubs tumbled over each other in their eagerness, the irksome flies forgotten for once. The pride began to see patches of grass that had been burnt by the fierce heat of the sun. In some places the ground smoked slightly. Tatu found a small snake, half in and half out of its burrow, which had been blackened by fire. It had been overtaken by flames before it could escape. There had been other deaths too. Slow-moving or otherwise vulnerable animals such as the lame or the very old had failed to survive the sporadic conflagrations. The lions saw a group of hyenas making a meal off one victim.

The smell of burnt meat was strong, but the fires seemed to have been selective in their choice of area. The burnt patches were confined to the places where shorter grasses had grown, and by no means all of these were affected. Some were small areas, some extensive. In a few spots flames still flickered, but the strong wind that had at first driven them had died away and all the small fires were burning themselves out. But there was a warning here for every inhabitant of the game park. Fire could strike again at any time.

The conditions were perfect. Abnormally high temperatures, dried-out vegetation; each day succeeding the one before without the slightest hint of any change to cooler or damper weather.

'Be careful where you tread,' Huru cautioned the cubs. 'Follow me exactly.' She threaded her way between the affected parts, feeling the ground anxiously with her paws and avoiding black or ashy tracts. The heat from the latter was severe. Eventually she found some meat. A full-grown gnu that had been unable to keep up with its departing herd had got caught in some thick thorn scrub which had been surrounded by various small fires. Huru found a way in to the prey and the trapped animal's misery was soon ended. With Kimya's help the lioness dragged the carcass clear and the pride settled down to eat.

When appetites were satisfied the sisters had time to reflect on what they had seen around them. The cubs were sleepy and lay down near their mothers to be licked clean. Huru and Kimya looked at the scorched landscape.

'This is the start of something, isn't it?' Kimya suggested.

'I think so,' Huru replied. 'All the signs are that we're in for a very dangerous time. We should keep the cubs around us always.'

'Yes. They mustn't wander.'

Huru was thinking of Moja and Battlescars. The sisters had no idea what had happened since the confrontation with the other lions. Now the threat of fire was an additional worry. Her thoughts were interrupted.

'Did you notice, sister,' Kimya was saying, 'there were no flies around this animal?' She meant the gnu.

'No, it didn't occur to me. But, now you mention it, I can see there are fewer flies round here altogether. They must be affected by fire the same as the rest of us.'

'Perhaps fire does bring some benefits, then.'

'I wish it would bring Moja and old Battlescars back to us,' said Huru.

There had been outbreaks of fire near fig tree rock too. Moja and his father had watched them from their makeshift den. Pembe had moved closer to the rock as the fires became more prevalent. And the honey badgers wondered yet again whether to move their quarters in the face of another potential danger.

'Difficult to see where else we could go that would be any better,' said Ratel.

'Somewhere without lions, at least,' Clicker suggested. 'That big male was sniffing around our entrance hole again last night. If he could get in here, he would. The goshawk was bad enough but we did know it couldn't eat *us*.'

'I know, I know,' Ratel agreed. 'The lion cub told me he was urging his father to move. Now there's the threat of burning, I think he may be successful. Why would he want to stay?'

Moja found some fire victims in the bush and told Battlescars about them. 'I ate what I needed,' he said. 'Why don't you fill your own stomach while there's a chance?'

'You know I don't leave this place except when it's dark,' Moja was reminded.

'But you're all but healed now,' the cub pointed out. 'And there were scarcely any flies where I went.'

'Is that so?' Battlescars pricked up his ears. 'I yearn for a proper feed, I must say.'

'Well, don't delay. There must be many hungry mouths like yours. The meat won't lie about for long, that's for sure.'

Battlescars got to his feet. His stomach rumbled in anticipation. 'I'll go with you,' he decided. 'Take me to it.'

Moja regretted the need to make another journey. He was tired. But he wanted his father to move away from the rocky shelter permanently, and he thought the reduction in insect numbers would be a good incentive. When they reached the place where Moja had fed there was little left of the remains. Battlescars grumbled but realised it was inevitable.

'The woodland pride,' he surmised in a mutter to himself, 'if they've still got the strength to eat.' He took what scraps there were and then wandered about in a search for more. Thinking about rivals led him to thoughts of his own pride. For a long time the lionesses and the other cubs had hardly been in his mind. He had been preoccupied with his own discomfort. Now at last the veil of self-absorption was lifting.

'Moja!' he called to his faithful son. 'You were right! I can live with this. We should bring the others back here; give them some relief too. We can make it our base. The woodland pride won't interfere with us.' He found some meat that had been overlooked and munched it contentedly.

Moja said, 'What about the fires? There may be more.'

Battlescars glanced around at the blackened areas. 'No fires now,' he grunted. 'Besides, it may be worse elsewhere.' He finished his meal. 'Let's drink,' he said. 'And then we'll find our pride.'

Moja sighed with relief. He longed to get away from this place and he was confident that Huru and Kimya would have no desire to return to fig tree rock.

In the dregs of the marsh area Moja and Battlescars came across Pembe, trying to cool himself. There was little water here but there was enough to drink. Battlescars paid little attention to the young rhino but Moja wanted to tell him his news.

'My father wants to collect the rest of the pride and bring them back here,' he explained. Battlescars was far enough from them for Moja to add, 'But I don't think he's strong enough. So we may not see each other for a while.'

Pembe snorted as he finished his drink. 'I wish you well wherever you are,' he said. 'I'll probably remain hereabouts. At least I know I can satisfy my thirst.'

'Yes. That's good,' Moja said. 'I don't think we've seen the last of the fires. It's as dry as dust everywhere. You can almost sense there's more to come.'

'Well, whether there is or not,' said Pembe, 'there's nothing we can do about it.' He bent his horned head to Moja's level. 'Whatever happens, take care,' he added feelingly.

'I will,' Moja answered. 'You must too.'

Battlescars was ready to move. The two young animals parted and the lions continued their journey. After a while Moja looked back. Pembe was watching him wistfully. He seemed so alone. Moja tried to shake the idea away. He had to think of his family first.

As they trudged over the sun-baked ground with its sparse, brittle vegetation Battlescars and Moja found evidence of fire everywhere. Smoke, ash and embers could be seen all around in scorched pockets of landscape. Far from there being a prospect of a respite from the merciless sun, it seemed to the lions to be hotter than ever. Battlescars's head sank lower and lower as they plodded into the endless glare. There was no breeze of any kind. The stillness all around was uncanny. There was hardly a sound from beast or bird. It was as though the entire game park, together with its occupants, was holding its breath while it waited helplessly for Nature to decide its fate. Moja kept behind his father, glad of the morsel of protection provided by Battlescars's body. The old male's pace became slower and slower. Just as he had decided to slump down in the first patch of shade they came to he saw Huru padding towards him. She had seen him and their cub from a distance.

Battlescars stood still as Huru greeted him, butting him and rubbing her head against his, her body brushing against his flanks. He responded gladly and then it was Moja's turn. The cub was delighted to see his mother and closed his eyes in sheer pleasure as she licked him lovingly.

'We hoped you would come,' she purred. 'We should be together at a time like this.'

'Yes,' Battlescars replied. 'That's why we're here.'

Minutes later the pride was complete again. They examined one another, sad to see the signs of their recent ordeal on each other. They told their stories and together they found a piece of shade where they lay down in a cluster. Moja was surrounded by his brother and sister and cousins. They made more of him than the big male.

'Later, when it's cooled off, I'll take you back,' Battlescars told them. 'Darkness is kinder to us all.'

'Back? Back to what?' the cubs asked their mothers.

It was Moja who answered them. 'He means back to the rocks.'

'I'm not moving anywhere,' Kimya said distinctly. 'And neither are my cubs.'

'No,' Huru agreed, but with some reluctance. 'There's no need, Battlescars.'

'There *is* need,' he insisted. 'I prefer it and it's much more comfortable. There are far fewer flies and—'

'There are fewer here too,' Kimya interrupted. She

was angry. 'You didn't worry about us when you were skulking in the rocks and we managed without you. We can do so again.'

There was silence for a long moment. The cubs wondered how the old male would react. But Battlescars no longer enjoyed the supreme dominance over other lions, male and female, he once had done. He knew he couldn't enforce his ideas. Before he could answer Huru tried to smooth his way.

'We really didn't gain anything by making the trek there before, did we?' she suggested. 'We're all too tired to make it again, especially since we'd gain nothing by it. We should keep together now. That means staying here on the plains.'

Battlescars had already noticed how scanty the flies had become here too. 'Very well,' he said graciously. 'The last thing I want is to see the pride broken up again.'

Kimya looked at Huru appreciatively but with some envy. She had to accept Huru's greater influence with the big male.

The major part of the day had gone. The pride dozed. Then suddenly all the lions were wide awake. A sharp *crack* like gunshot had them all scrambling to their feet. In the distance they saw a deep glow of red. Though they couldn't see smoke, the smell of it was in their nostrils. A bigger, hungrier fire was approaching, snapping off small trees as it advanced across the already scorched ground. A rustle, a hiss, the sigh of grasses engulfed by flame were distinctly audible.

Battlescars said, 'Now, if we're to save our skins, we have a trek to make whether we like it or not.'

14

Purification

The question was, where to go for safety? It was difficult to see from which direction the fire was approaching. The cubs were frightened and their instinct was to run instantly. The adults managed to calm them. Battlescars still thought the best plan was to make for the rocky shelter.

'How do we know there isn't fire over there?' Kimya asked tensely.

'We don't, but we have to move somewhere. Look!' Battlescars saw how the fire was driving animals before it. On all sides groups of gazelles, topis and other smaller mammals such as hares, mongooses, porcupines and a lone warthog were running blindly as the *whoosh* of the flames sounded at their backs. The lions saw their eyes were wide with terror and this communicated itself to them. They broke into a run. Huru and Kimya tried to keep the cubs together. A leopard with her own cub bounded past them and the noise of the fire increased. A savage crackling as the flames consumed everything in their path grew steadily louder. Animal cries and the screeches of birds were added to the din and now smoke came billowing on a current of air impelled by the fire. Huru darted a glance behind. She was in the rear of the pride and, ahead of the intensifying red glow, she saw another male lion galloping towards her. She recognised him at once as the brave young lion who had challenged Battlescars.

Challenger was able to run faster than the lionesses, who were impeded by their need to care for the cubs. He caught Huru up and panted hoarsely, 'It's all around! The whole area is in flames. Run for your lives!'

The dark sky was illuminated by fireglow, a lurid light that made familiar objects look unreal. The game park's inhabitants were in a panic. Some ran one way only to find flames there before them. Then, doubling back, turning, twisting, they tried to find a way through to safety elsewhere. The lions heard the desperate trumpeting of elephants, the yelling of hyenas and alarm cries of baboons. All were caught up in a mad rush to escape but most animals ran without thought, crossing and criss-crossing the ground, unable to reason or see ahead.

The flames, finding no barrier, accelerated. Slower beasts were caught in the fire's cruel embrace before they knew it was upon them. Battlescars was tiring. He began to drop back as Huru, Kimya and the cubs increased their speed. Moja tried to keep his father in view, but it was difficult to turn his head as he ran and each time he did manage to look Battlescars was even farther behind. The old lion urged him not to hesitate, panting, 'Go on, son. Save yourself. I'll catch you up later.'

Huru saw Upesi and one of her cubs far ahead and she tried to keep them in view, seeming to draw strength from their speed. Kimya saw her pulling away and cried out.

'Sister! Don't leave me!' Even the cubs' vulnerability was forgotten in the most basic instinct for self-preservation. But Huru was checked. As Kimya drew level Challenger sprinted past and found time to feel a wisp of triumph, knowing Battlescars to be well behind. But it wasn't a race and Challenger knew no better than any other animal which was the safest course to run.

Upesi suddenly veered wildly and the lionesses saw a tongue of flame almost catch her from a direction where no fire had seemed to be before. There appeared to be no escape. The plains, long sucked dry of moisture, were alight. In the absence of any resistance, it was as though the whole landscape lay prostrate before a terrible conqueror. Only those creatures who had been forewarned and had had time to dive into deep burrows were not put to flight. A few quaked in rocky crevices or holes, not daring to move. Amongst these were Ratel and Clicker.

Huru's and Kimya's cubs had so far managed to keep close to their mothers. They saw them swerve to follow Upesi's track. Suddenly Moja knew there was only one way they could be sure of escaping death. The river! If they could just get to its near bank, it surely would require no great feat to cross it after the long weeks of drought. However low the water now, it might suffice to present the vital barrier to the fire's progress. He tried to assess their surroundings. In the semi-darkness and in the first throes of panic none of the lions had taken any stock of where they were heading. Now Moja was astonished to see that they were running, after all, towards a rocky outcrop that he recognised as fig tree rock, where Battlescars had wanted to go all along. He could get some kind of bearing from that. He looked again for his father but now Battlescars couldn't be seen at all. Moja gasped to Huru with what little breath he had to spare, 'Mother! The river! It's our only chance.'

Huru turned momentarily without slackening her

pace. The flames threatened to encircle them but there was one narrow channel ahead that was clear and Moja spurted past Huru towards it. Many of the other animals had taken different directions. It was impossible to tell if they had escaped or been consumed. The lion pride was almost alone. Challenger had disappeared; so had Upesi. Moja saw a bulky animal looming to his right, seeming to have given up any attempt to survive. It was Pembe, who had been stupefied by heat and was standing still, waiting for the flames to claim him. Moja tried to call to his friend, and managed to croak, 'Pembe! Come with us!'

The rhino blinked and his heavy body shook as he came to his senses. He began to lumber towards the exhausted pride.

The lions passed through the gap. They could feel the scorching breath of the fire on their pelts, but they kept just ahead of the tongues of flame, some of which were beginning to lick around the honey badgers' rocky shelter. And now the roar of the inferno was constantly in the pride's ears. It was like a voice that bellowed at them from all sides, as if made furious by their efforts to outdistance it. Moja didn't know how he kept running. The other cubs were close to collapse. Huru and Kimya were side by side, mute, deafened and without thought. But the river bank at last came into view. Moja threw himself over the rim and tumbled down towards the narrow, muddy channel of water. He remembered Pembe and Kifaru and their walk across, and found himself up to his neck in the river with his feet just able to touch the bottom. He was too exhausted to swim and stayed where he was. Mbili, Nne and Tano came next with the lionesses. Huru and Kimya waded through the river, lapping at the water greedily as they crossed.

Sita joined the other cubs at the river's edge. Moja saw that his sister Tatu was missing just as a burst of flame rushed up to the lip of the bank. Tatu seemed to be in the middle of it and she was howling. All at once a huge bulky creature appeared behind her, lowered its head and butted her into the water. Pembe had saved her and Moja willed him to save himself. The fire had caught the rhino but he blundered on and slammed on to his side near the cubs. Steam rose from his body as the river lapped at him. His tail and rump were burnt but he was alive.

The cubs watched in trepidation as the flames hovered above them. Fire began to creep down the bank. Huru and Kimya called repeatedly, 'Youngsters, you must swim. Come across, come across.'

The cubs hesitated. Moja was looking along the bank as far as it was possible to see, seeking his father once more, but Battlescars was nowhere in evidence. Finally he turned and began to paddle. The other cubs followed suit and soon rejoined their mothers. The flames flickered, reaching out once more for Pembe, but the rhino stirred, hauled himself to his feet and slowly, snorting with relief, lumbered across. He was not badly burnt and the water soothed his seared hindquarters. Lions and Pembe stood together silently. On the other side of the river the fire raged unchecked. It seemed to the watchers that the whole world, their world, was in flames.

The lions waited in vain for their old pride leader. They knew only a miracle could save him. But there was no miracle and at last, full of sorrow, they accepted that Battlescars's age had told against him. He was lost to them for ever.

The fire burnt for two days. The national government chartered aircraft with firefighting equipment and tons of water were dropped in an attempt to halt the flames' destruction. On the ground the military was called in to create firebreaks to contain the blazes where possible. Everyone from Kamenza assisted, Simon and Joel working side by side, masked and muffled in protective clothing. They watched in horror as the fire's grip, despite all their efforts, barely slackened. And it wasn't until Nature's mood changed that the flames finally surrendered. A violent thunderstorm unleashed enough rain to douse the fire entirely. The savannah was left smoking and steaming, blackened and scarred almost beyond recognition where once there had been wide swaths of grassland. Many animals were lost; Simon Obagwe was heartbroken. But the game park had been purged. The plague of flies had vanished, obliterated completely by heat, smoke and flame.

The Obagwe family, together with Joel, looked out at the devastation. Through his field glasses Simon watched some of the surviving game pick its way through burnt vegetation and ashy soil. Some areas had remained untouched by the disaster and the grazers and browsers found their way there.

'Can you see our lions?' Annie hardly dared to ask. 'Are they alive still, Daddy?'

'I can't see them just now,' he answered. 'But there were lions beyond the river and they must have survived because the fire didn't reach that far.'

'Were there cubs?'

'Yes, cubs too.'

'Were they . . . were they . . .?' Annie began.

Her father read her thoughts. 'Joel and I will go to look,' he assured her, 'just as soon as we can. We have to make a circuit of the entire park to see what animals are left.'

*

When the rains began in earnest, new green shoots began to appear through the sooty remains of the previous season. The great herds would return when it was time. Meanwhile, the resident species recognised signs of new life and were glad. Huru and Kimya had seen all their cubs survive and the pride thrived, although as yet no male had appeared on the scene to replace Battlescars. Kimya wondered about Challenger, but she didn't concern herself too much about his fate. If he had escaped the fire he would come looking for them. And if he came looking for them he would find two sister lionesses so devoted to each other and so moulded by their experiences together that it would be impossible to separate them. He would also find amongst the sturdy cubs one Moja, halfway to independence, who would one day be ready to challenge for his own pride elsewhere. The youngster's temperament had been well and truly tested by his gruelling experiences and had not been found lacking. Some of his father's old stature was beginning to show in the son. And Moja thought constantly of Battlescars; the old lion's strength and courage were his model. His father would never be forgotten.

Gradually the scars on the landscape healed. The game park took on a new coat of green. Simon and Joel had scoured the park and were encouraged by the numbers of game remaining in it. Losses, although extensive, were not as severe as they had at one time feared. Already there had been some new births. There was still much to be hopeful about. Nature was the key to the park's recovery and they must rely on her to work its salvation. But they could help, and one afternoon they were relaxing at the refuge centre after dealing with the release of the young female rhino into the bush. During this operation they had seen Huru and Kimya hunting, then the whole pride feeding from a kill. Now they waited for Annie to come home from school so that they could take her and Emelda to see the lion family together.

'Youngsters,' Joel murmured. 'They're the future, aren't they? And the game park treasures its young just as we do.'

JOURNEY to FREEDOM

Colin Dann

Lingmere Zoo is closing and its twin lionesses, Lorna and Ellen, will be put down unless a new home can be found for them. So when a sanctuary in Africa offers to take the animals, they begin the long journey together. But Lorna wants her freedom and she escapes into the English countryside leaving Ellen to face an unknown fate, alone. Can the lionesses survive without each other in their frightening new worlds? And will they ever meet again?

The first book
in the fantastic
LIONS OF LINGMERE
SERIES
£3.99 0099403447

LION COUNTRY

Colin Dann

The twin lionesses transported from
Lingmere Zoo to an African sanctuary
have been renamed. Ellen has become
Kimya, which means quiet, and Lorna is Huru,
meaning free. Released into the wild, they are
forced to fend for themselves as they face
hunger, unbearable heat and, worst of all,
the deadly wrath of the other animals.
Will the sisters survive to create a new pride?

The second book
in the fantastic
LIONS OF LINGMERE
SERIES

£3.99 0099407779

RED FOX STORY COLLECTIONS

If you are looking for a little animal magic then these brilliant bind-ups bring you stories of every creature, great and small. There are the fantastic creatures that Doctor Dolittle lives and works with in **DOCTOR DOLITTLE STORIES**, the bold and brave animals described in **ANIMAL STORIES** and there are three memorable tales of horse riding and friendship in **PONY STORIES**.

DOCTOR DOLITTLE STORIES
by Hugh Lofting
Selected stories from the Doctor Dolittle Books
0 09 926593 1 £4.99

ANIMAL STORIES
The Winged Colt of Casa Mia by Betsy Byars
Stories from Firefly Island by Benedict Blathwayt
Farthing Wood, The Adventure Begins
by Colin Dann
0 09 926583 4 £4.99

PONY STORIES
A Summer of Horses by
Carol Fenner
Fly-by-Night by K. M. Peyton
Three to Ride by Christine
Pullein-Thompson
0 09 940003 0 £4.99